METAL STORM
Weird Custer
a Novel

By William H. Sumrall

SHANTI PUBLISHING

ISBN: 978-0692381786

10 9 8 7 6 5 4 3 2 1

1st Edition, February 2015

Shanti Publishing

1970 Hanalima St U-206

Lihue, HI 96766

« Chapter One »

THE BROAD EXPANSE of the Montana Territory lay stretched in an emerald green sea of grass before them under the gleaming sun. As they disappeared into the broad distance, those who remained in the rear had the impression that the streams of mounted cavalry were being swallowed into an ocean of tall grass. The vista appeared to the mounted soldiers like an unbroken series of rolling, undulating grassy expanses. The grasses were a rich mix of rough fescue, junegrass and oatgrass. Sagebrush was abundant and emitted a sweet, cloying odor when trampled by the horses.

Into the unexplored Montana Territory rode Lieutenant Colonel Custer at the head of the 7th Cavalry. He was a blond haired man of many strengths and weaknesses, a man whose aspirations knew no limits.

They made 12 miles up the Rosebud River before dusk, riding hard. The former general halted the columns of horse soldiers. Seeing about him a great pastureland, Custer ordered his command, covered in dust and worn raw, to dismount and make camp. The lean, powerfully built officer stood up in the stirrups and looked all around him as he assessed the immediate vicinity. The ridiculously wide straw hat was pulled low over the brow, shielding his eyes from the angle of the setting sun. Custer studied several hills nearby where he could place lookouts. He sat back down on the saddle once more, holding the reins of Vic, his favorite horse, with one hand and holding the saddle horn with the other; he turned and spoke to his brother Thomas. He twisted at his waist to face his brother, turning his head sharply to his left as he did so not wishing to disturb the position of his one thousand pound gelding as it grazed the lush grass.

"X marks the spot! We'll call it a day here and set up bivouac! Tom, you and Calhoun place the companies along the water's edge, but don't spread out too much. Have the securities tripled."

The horizon was still illuminated in a spectacular wash of orange vexed with hot red, although the sun had set behind the distant Bighorn Mountains. Already Venus was glowing brightly above the horizon as Jupiter and Saturn appeared high overhead, preceding the stars by thirty minutes or so. The ever-present wolves, often invisible but always nearby, were beginning to howl, answered by the ubiquitous yelps of their smaller cousins, the coyotes. The Boy General had felt a premonition of gloom that he sought to dispel after he had summoned all of his officers.

"Wop! Sound Officer's Call!" yelled Custer.

Giovani Martini placed the brass trumpet to his lips and blasted the melody from the instrument. The high pitched notes rang from the brass trumpet, and carried for miles in the waning penumbral moments. The wolves and coyotes responded in a cacophony of howls and yelps, and were answered by their shaggy brethren from miles away.

The orange taper of the coal oil lantern flickered dubiously in the command tent of the former general, now demoted to lieutenant colonel, as his orders drew on into the night. The lantern threw a semicircle of ambient light on the five men who stood about a field table, on which lay an incomplete map of the land into which they were headed. Custer leaned over the map, pointing with the index finger of his right hand at the position of their current location. The other four figures leaned forward, following the imaginary line being drawn by their commanding officer as he traced a route toward the unexplored valley of the Little Bighorn River. They strained to see in the soft, orange glow of the coal oil lamp suspended from the single tent pole as it sputtered.

"We are to go it alone into that unexplored wilderness?" expostulated a small, chubby man of middle years who stood directly across the field table from the lieutenant colonel. There was apprehension in his voice.

"This is unprecedented," continued the chubby man. "We may as well be chasing a Will o' the Wisp."

"Who asked for your opinion?" was the response of the commanding officer, whose steely blue eyes bore into the doubtful officer.

Custer's eyes narrowed into slits to better focus his sight in the wavering lantern light as he looked back down upon the map which lay before them. He explained the order of march and described with some detail the lay of the land into which they were going. This information had been provided to him by his Indian scouts, which he used to embellish the rudimentary map they surrounded.

"By Jove!" uttered the older, clean shaven man to Custer's left. "We will be entering unexplored territory, and can name various mountains and ridges after the officers who stand about this table."

A sharp glance from the commanding officer muted any further utterance from the Army captain. The tall blond man stepped back from the table as he changed the subject from the map to what he expected of his key officers. He seemed to be nervous, unable to focus his train of thought as he continued with the order.

"It is my desire to impress upon you the necessity of following my orders implicitly; there will be no trumpet calls, except in cases of most dire urgency. Extraordinary orders are to be cleared with me personally. Riding at the front of the column, I shall elect upon which site to set camp, and when to break the same..."

The officers in the roomy tent were uneasy; uncertainties of plunging into the unknown gave rise to gnawing questions that had to be asked. Thomas Custer, the former general's younger brother waited until the order was complete, and was the first to ask a question. Thomas glanced at his companions, whose eyes were focused on their host. Their common sense might have deterred them from plunging headlong into the unknown, but potential charges of desertion made them follow orders. He looked to his older brother as he postulated the question.

"How far do we march tomorrow? The horses are worn and the men exhausted. At some point we need to ease up the pace at which we're going. At this rate the 7th will be spent before we make contact."

Custer sat down on his cot, removing his boots. He looked haggard and older than his 36 years. Although a physically fit and vigorous man at 36, he suffered from a number of ailments. He endured short-windedness from numerous respiratory complications, and suffered from shingles, and incapacitating migraine headaches. An infection of gonorrhea had plagued him since his West Point days as a cadet.

"Rest easy, men. I'll answer all your questions. Tom, we will push as far and as fast as we can tomorrow. Crook is probably in contact with them now, or will be by tomorrow. I have it on good word that there are a large number of hostiles, and Crook is going to need our help or else risk high casualties. Does that answer your question?"

Unbeknownst to Army Headquarters, General Crook's offensive had been defeated in a six hour battle extending over a three mile front. Rather than pressing onward into Big Sky Country, Crook cited depleted ammunition and supplies as the primary reason to not pursue the Sioux and Cheyenne. Doubtful of surviving another attack, he withdrew to an area near Sheridan, Wyoming. Crook remained there impotently for seven weeks awaiting supplies, licking his wounds like a whipped dog.

An up and coming Sioux warrior whose star was on the rise had orchestrated the defeat of Crook, which would inflict cataclysmic repercussions on Custer. The painted Crazy Horse, a charismatic and gifted leader flushed with triumph, was rushing with thousands of warriors to link up with the venerable Sitting Bull, who had predicted their victory. Crazy Horse wore no bonnet, nor did he wear paint on his forehead. He wore a yellow lightning bolt down the left side of his face. He would dampen white talc and paint hailstones on vulnerable parts of his body and in conjunction with proper medicine he believed himself bulletproof.

Crazy Horse was a veteran of many battles with the US Army, being present at the battle of Platte Bridge, and Red Buttes, as well as the Fetterman Massacre, and at the Wagon Box fight. He was a shirt wearer, who had been stripped of this title in disgrace for sleeping with another man's wife. Although he didn't wear the shirt in battle, he had earned the right to wear it; it was a symbol of honor, important to have at ceremonial gatherings. The war shirt was unique to the owner, and decorated with beads, bones and small bells which made a stunning display of sight and sound at the war dances. Crazy Horse never forgave the cuckolded husband. Despite this stain upon his reputation, never before had the forces of the Sioux shown such discipline and cohesion as they had under the command of Crazy Horse.

The amulets and feathered headdresses were meticulously blessed by Sitting Bull, making the wearer believe he was bullet proof. Sitting Bull was the Hunkpapa Lakota holy man who the chiefs looked to for wisdom, guidance, and sorcery. In 1875 Sitting Bull and the Cheyenne medicine man White Bull, along with their combined tribes came together for the Sun Dance. The magic was enhanced by the self-mutilation of Sitting Bull, in which he cut off one hundred pieces of flesh from his thickly muscled arms to offer as sacrifice to his deities, deities spoken of only in hushed whispers inside darkened tepees. Witkokaga the Befooler would be pulled out of vast distances over nameless gulfs. Gulfs that transcended time and space. Witkokaga the Befooler, the Shapeshifter, Wood Nymph, Demoness, High Priestess: Witkokaga was all of these things and many more, but for the goddess to answer the priest who summoned her, there would be a heavy price. A heavy price to pay for the Holy Man who summoned her.

Sitting Bull's combat experience lent itself to the dual role of a chief; he saw numerous actions in Red Cloud's War. He had led almost continual attacks on wagon trains of immigrants, surveying parties and forts, such as Forts Berthold, Stevenson and Buford.

But it was Sitting Bull's magic that temporarily halted the progress of the railroad penetration into tribal lands. Through the use of horrific human sacrifices of captive immigrants he created The Panic of 1873. This financial crisis triggered an economic depression in North America and Europe that had repercussions for the next twenty years. Thousands of Native American fighting men were being blessed by Sitting Bull, White Bull and medicine men who possessed less powerful magic, such as Black Elk, who was a twelve year old prodigy and second cousin to Crazy Horse.

It was only the braves who violated the myriad stipulations inherent to the magic that seemed to be blasted out of their saddles, to die horribly as they were drug behind their mounts with a foot hung in a stirrup. Stirrups of saddles atop horses that differed profoundly from those of the cavalry sent to engage their riders. The much smaller Indian ponies were of mixed origins, having pedigree in the Arabian breeds brought over to Spain during the Muslim invasion. Later, these horses were cross bred with Barb and Andalusian stock.

"Ah, yes, General, I have no further questions, for now." Thomas saw that several of the other men had resumed looking at the map.

Reno was the next to speak. He was ill at ease with Custer's unusual demeanor. Oval faced with a straight nose, underneath which resided a neatly trimmed moustache, Major Marcus Reno was a pudgy man, growing stout in middle age.

"Sir, McDougal is only now arriving with the pack train. He is constantly far behind us, and I think this endangers us all, in the event we make contact with a large war party. Perhaps I could suggest someone else for the job."

Custer stood barefoot, and walked to a pewter basin and began washing his hands, then taking a wash cloth, began wiping the trail dust from his face and eyes.

"McDougal has a hard task. He's doing as good as, and probably better than, anyone else would. He pushes his men and animals hard, and doesn't take any shit. What I'll do is have him leave ahead of us in the morning. Detach two of your squads to give him additional security. When we pass him, your squads will reattach with your element. When we make camp tomorrow, you will go further ahead with Bloody Knife and get an eye for what's out there. Terry has a high degree of confidence in your ability to assess the lay of the land. Then I mean to send Varnum far in advance and won't have discourse with him as soon as I'd like. What else? Ask away."

"Sir, I have not another question, and your orders merit admiration," ejaculated Reno, in a sycophantic tone.

The import of Major Reno's response was not missed by the Boy General. And after a pause, Custer responded with pent up hostility which he had hidden from Reno, but which he now set free. He turned on Reno, his light complexioned skin turning red with restrained fury. This could be seen in the unsteady lantern light as the wick grew shorter. The uncertain light served to highlight the shadows and exaggerate the surly expressions of the general's face as he spoke.

"General Terry expressly insisted that you conduct this reconnaissance. That's the only reason you have the mission, instead of me. You had better give me an accurate assessment of what lies ahead," continued Custer.

There was tense silence in the tent for a moment, then it was broken by the liquid sound of water being wrung from the bath cloth as the droplets rained back into the basin.

"Or I will have your ass! Do you understand me, Major Reno?"

Reno's heart palpitated and the palms of his hands itched as he stood to attention and responded, "Yes, sir!"

Custer removed his shirt and began cleaning his arms with the washcloth, then his armpits. He immersed the cloth into the already brown water and wrung the sweat and grime from the rag, then began cleaning his lean, muscular chest with it.

"What about you, Captain? You look like you have something special on your mind."

Captain Benteen studied the man before him with contempt.

"Nope, Lt. Colonel," he said with emphasis, omitting the respectful title of General, which he knew Custer craved.

"I understand very well," continued Benteen, taking advantage of Custer's hurt ego. Benteen exploited the barb, sinking it in and twisting it like a knife. The captain, seeking to open the wound even more, pressed his attack. "We wouldn't want Ol' Varnum to get too far ahead, now would we? I'd hate to see him face overwhelming odds and no one be around to help."

The brown bath cloth was immersed into the water again, and re-emerged once more. The droplets of water falling back into the bowl were all that could be heard in the deafening silence that followed. Custer wrung the filthy water from it and washed the sweat from his private parts as he spoke to Benteen.

"Yes, you do have a valid concern, don't you, Captain?"

Benteen was a talented and experienced officer who had more going against him than not having attended West Point. Years before, he had crossed Custer, embarrassing him in a newspaper column and then calling his bluff openly in front of his officers. As Custer prepared to strike him with a whip, Benteen placed his hand on his service revolver. The result was that Custer backed off, hinting that the topic would be addressed later. And it would be, over and over again. Benteen could never leave the command of Custer, and Custer never allowed Benteen to be promoted. The ongoing personal animosity between the two was known to the whole command, which for the most part disliked both of the individuals.

Once this campaign is seen to completion, I will soon be president, Custer thought to himself *and I will ruin this man. I will see him drummed out of the Army on some trumped up charge.*

The snide address as "Captain" had stung Benteen. The feud between the two officers went back to an incident that had occurred nearly nine years before. The 7th had attacked Cheyenne Chief Black Kettle's Southern winter camp on the Washita River in the Oklahoma Territory. Black Kettle's camp was the westernmost of a formidable string of villages consisting of Cheyenne, Arapaho, Kiowa, Comanche, and even Apache bands, running nearly twenty miles up the Washita River.

What had initially started as a punitive expedition to preempt further raiding parties against settlers, turned into a fight for survival against overwhelming odds. Benteen's close personal friend, Major Joel Elliot, along with twenty men, had been abandoned and left behind by an unnerved Custer. Elliot's detachment had been butchered and many in the 7th never forgave Custer. Benteen, in particular, bitterly hated Custer for this action.

"Yellow Hair! They call him! Thought Frederick Benteen to himself. *Yellow as piss! That is what that dog is!* He felt the blood rushing to his ears as he fought down the urge to talk back, to insult. The

repetitive splashing of the soiled rag into the bowl of filthy water distracted Benteen, as he became aware for the first time of how filthy he himself was. *Damned West Pointers! How I hate them! How I hate them all!* His mental rage restrained behind his lips in the form of a scowl as the water splashed in the basin. "Pilate washed his hands, too." Muttered Benteen, suddenly alarmed that he had spoken aloud, and preparing himself for the response he knew would come.

Custer dropped the rag into the basin and turned to face the captain. His features were distorted into a mask of fury, reminding Benteen of an enraged mountain lion. His voice was high pitched, with a Midwest accent. He stammered as he spoke.

"This borderline belligerence will be addressed, Captain, but now is not the time or the place to settle old scores." The commanding officer advanced on his subordinate, who looked down involuntarily at the general's penis. It was shrunken in the chill night air and dripped a foul smelling mucous discharge of gonorrhea. It oozed and suspended a strand of the bacteria laden exudate fully to the bullet scar on the general's left thigh before detaching itself and falling to the earth.

« Chapter Two »

OUTSIDE, THE EVENING had drawn into chilled night, and the stars flickered wickedly as the lantern sputtered within the tent, casting uncertain shadows within its walls. The canvas walls of the tent would billow from time to time with a gust of breeze. The breeze carried with it the howling of wolves and coyotes, from near and far. These sounds of the night seemed to fade once Custer resumed oratory as he completed his physical hygiene.

"The Gatling guns would have been cumbersome and dead weight, serving only to slow us down. I have seen their demonstrations and can avow that the realization of a few spins of the barrels would see them most fouled, the bores being so choked with spent powder residue as to render them useless. As to want of a further battalion of cavalry, that is completely unneeded–the 7th needs not the help of sister commands; we can handle this matter of the Sioux and Cheyenne forthwith. I appeal to you to take pride in your regiment; the best the Army has yet fielded." stated Custer, in a matter of fact way, to his stunned audience. Done with his bath, the former general momentarily eschewed shirt and britches, but later he would sleep attired; in the event of an attack, so that he would not be hampered with nudity. Custer believed every word he said, not caring whether his subordinates thought so or not.

The yellow haired man paused, absent mindedly to pull back his curled locks, remembering in a flash of a moment that he had recently cut his hair short. He was for the day, a tall man, two inches short of standing six feet, lean and muscular. Cobalt blue eyes which often held an accusing gaze lurked menacingly in the handsome face. His overlong well-formed nose extended above a thick, drooping blond moustache. His blond hair–renowned for falling to his shoulders in lustrous curls, was shorn short for purposes of hygiene and practicality. His hairline receded savagely at the temples, thrusting the tongue of a pronounced widow's peak through the center.

Captain Benteen regarded Lieutenant Colonel Custer with nauseating repugnance, but with a slap of his riding crop on the side of his boot and a nod of his head acquiesced to Custer's authority. Uneasy and surprised by the unusual monologue and yet another close brush with disaster, he withheld his speculations from Reno as they walked from the candle lit tent into the darkness.

"That whole episode was off canter," remarked Reno. "I've not seen him to speak in such manner afore. The whole parlance was odd, indeed. So out of character with the man; the excessive instructions, explanations, the pleading–for such an egotist–damned odd!"

Under hushed breath, Benteen warned Reno lower his voice, lest the two brothers in the tent overhear. Captain Frederick Benteen was a man of average build and thick, graying hair, atop a high forehead and a cherubic, smooth shaven face.

"Shhhh! Shut your mouth you damned milk-sop, or I'll shut it for you, permanently!" Benteen hissed.

"You had best stop addressing me in such a manner, Captain!" retorted the surprised Reno, whereupon Benteen rammed the haft of his riding crop forcefully into the gut of Reno, causing him to double over, then struck him across the back of the head, knocking him down.

"Your damned West Point ring won't get you any points out here, Major!" Benteen's effort to maintain his whisper had failed, and Thomas Custer opened the flap of the tent, illuminating the scene of the captain assisting the major up.

"The Major just had a misstep is all, that's all there is to it, Tom!" assured Captain Benteen confidently.

For a second Thomas Custer thought he caught a beam of humor in the leprechaun face of Benteen, then he turned back to speak with his elder sibling.

16

As he let go of the tent flap, darkness engulfed the Montana Territory once more.

Certainly not a coward, yet always relegated into the shadow of his brother, Captain Thomas Custer did not share in the same celebrity status. But neither was he an unknown in the profession of arms, nor was his potential lost on the political press. He had joined the Union Army at 16 years of age, having two times won the Medal of Honor-the first soldier to receive the medal twice. Like his brother, he had always exhibited a death wish; days before the War ended he'd been shot at point blank range in the face; the bullet had torn through the soft tissue of the mouth and exited at a point just below the right ear. Although quiet and withdrawn, resisting authority from other superior ranking officers, Thomas maintained a lapdog devotion to his brother that was often mistaken for servitude.

Thomas saw his brother pouring the filthy water of the wash basin onto the bare ground at the edge of the tent flap. He was troubled that all of the immediate members of the male family were present in this undertaking as he ran his hand through his dark, unwashed hair. The wavering shadows within the tent did little to assuage his concerns.

"What about Boston? I don't feel good about this one, Audie. Boston shouldn't be here; he's not cut out for this. I can't stop worrying about him." said Thomas, whose shadow was exaggerated against the canvas wall as the lantern bathed his chiseled features in soft yellow light.

Familial ties were not limited to a single member of the family, either. The 7th was rife with nepotism; the youngest brother served as quartermaster; "gofer" would be a better way to put it. Boston Custer's health prevented him from passing the Army physical and getting in. So the youngest brother performed myriad errands and chores, including guide, forager, packer, and scout. Boston shared the good looks of both his older brothers, and had a fresh, youthful appearance even at 28 years of age. This was at a time when a man could have appeared to be 50 at such an age.

"He'll be fine, Tom. Got him doing errands and important chores. The men obey him as they would an officer. I'll make sure he's in the rear with the gear before the shit hits the pan. I've got Harry in charge of herding the cattle, so he'll be out of the fracas as well. Things are under control as well as they can be, nothing's going to happen to this family. The Indian will always run when confronted by cavalry." reassured George Armstrong Custer, or "Audie" as those closest to him often referred to him.

Harry Armstrong Reed was a nephew of the three Custer brothers; he was the baby of the bunch, being only eighteen years old. His primary function was to herd the cattle that fed the regiment.

There was the sound of someone bumping into things in the dark outside the tent. Curse words caused Thomas to turn his head toward the entrance as Jimmy Calhoun opened the flap and entered. The shadow cast by Thomas' head was exaggerated on the tent wall as Calhoun entered the canvas structure. The sputtering of the lantern was lessened as the general turned the small brass knob lengthening the wick. The light increased noticeably. James "Jimmy" Calhoun was the brother in law married to the Custers' sister, Margaret. He was the commanding officer of Company L.

"Sorry for being late, I've got men that are down in the saddle with bad backs." said Calhoun, his surprise at seeing his brother in law naked was hidden in the gloomy light.

The truth was, Company L was ravaged with syphilis, and the hard ride had exacerbated the massive infection which had manifested itself in the urinary tracts leading through the bladder and into the kidneys.

"No mind. You'll ride lead in the morning, give your men and horses a break from the dust. How many do you figure are going to fall out?" asked Custer, whose minor movements were exaggerated on the wall of the tent, and seemed to shrink and grow with the ebb and gust of the prairie wind.

Custer was still naked, having finished his wash basin bath. He began putting his clothes back on. As he hiked up his trousers, his penis was jerked upward and a long strand of gonorrheal discharge flew from it, hitting the canvas wall of the tent. He would sleep in the clothing so that he could respond in a moment's notice if Indians attacked during the night, although he knew that was unlikely, it had happened before.

"Some two dozen would have already, had I not put the fear of God into them. I've not seen so many men poxed all at the same time before. It seems to be confined to my company, I've warned them about those Cree whores." answered Calhoun.

Calhoun was praised and kidded for his Adonis good looks. He married well, and came from a strong business family. He had never been of an amorous disposition, despite his handsome face and masculine body. The fact that he had married at all was based purely on practicality and what he considered a once in a lifetime opportunity to rise to spectacular heights with Custer's political future. The fact that his wife hated being touched and found the distinguishing part of male anatomy repulsive did not bother Jimmy. He had never had an erection at the sight of a woman and he felt that he had the perfect marriage. Perfect for himself and for Margaret. He thought about how fortunate he was that George had arranged the marriage between the two-two people with so much in common.

He was jolted back to the present when he heard Bloody Knife speak haltingly with Custer.

"More injun than Custer have bullet."

Custer began furiously speaking to his favorite scout and probably best friend in sign language.

Bloody Knife answered with a flurry of hand motions, both of them were gesticulating so wildly that Calhoun knew that there was a test of wills here, so powerful that he was mesmerized by the spectacle. Sweat beaded Bloody Knife's visage as he grimaced and contorted his face in tandem with the hand movements. Calhoun's respect for his brother in law increased at the sight of this duel of wills. He thanked his lucky stars that he was a member of the Custer family, lock, stock and barrel.

« Chapter Three »

DURING THE EARLY fall of 1875, George Armstrong Custer and his beautiful wife Elizabeth, were touring New York City, as the General was on an extended leave. Having addressed both the Century Society and the New York Historical Society, he agreed to give a series of lectures and caught the attention of very important men of political note–including James Gordon Bennet. Bennet was the son of a Scottish immigrant who made good on his immigration and founded the New York Herald. Bennet Sr. passed on his legacy to Bennet Jr. who was to urge Custer to run in the Presidential election coming late in 1876, and seconded by his cohort of influential friends, Custer warmed to the idea. Custer was on the fence about which party he would seek election under. Grant had split the Republican Party and his Reconstruction policies were in shambles. The charismatic Custer had always had sympathies with the South, even though he had been an instrument in their defeat.

Bennet, having met with Custer and speaking in confidence with him was unnerved by the steely intensity of Custer's probing blue eyes. Calculating, penetrating fire burned in those eyes as they narrowed. The celebrity soldier chuckled.

"There is nary a soul which could defeat me in the election of such an esteemed office." laughed George Armstrong Custer, whose tone was half serious, half joking. The laugh reminded Bennet of the deep purr of a mountain lion.

Custer had a rapid way of talking in a high pitched voice which was combined with a ridiculous farcical expression when he tried to inspire humor.

That will have to change the newspaper tycoon thought to himself. Custer seemed to read the mogul's mind and the stupid expression vanished, the tone of the voice sharpened and Custer neared uncomfortably close to the most powerful figure the press had ever known.

"Nary a soul, wouldn't you say?" reiterated the General, "milk-sops, effeminate dandies that call themselves men. Impersonators who made their way in life based on their father's connections." barbed Custer directly at Bennet, who sidestepped the insult. A career newspaper man, Bennet knew how to take a hit and not take things too personally. His was a world of jabs and counter jabs.

Bennet, though no coward, took a backward step before the sheer magnetic force of will that flowed in an interrogating scrutiny from Custer's eyes. The eyes made minor movements from left to right as they seemed to break through into the magnate's mind. James Gordon Bennet could feel the raw, naked ambition behind the azul eyes. The eyes of a man made mad by ambition, he thought.

Bennet was wearing a dark colored waist coat with a contrasting collar. A gold watch chain dangled conspicuously from one of the pockets. He wore a wide ascot tie and black, highly polished square toed shoes.

"It's not a done deal, you know. There's Sherman, Sheridan, Crook and a plethora of others." but Bennet knew Custer was his man and that he was going to pin his fortune on this rising star.

"They don't have it." countered Custer, "I started out as the son of a blacksmith, I earned my rank-nothing was ever given to me. I've risked my life a thousand times on the battlefield and have a thousand scars to show for it."

"Word has it that Grant's out to get you, General. Seems you embarrassed him rather recently." Bennet was walking on thin ice, but knew he had to do it if he were to gain the man's fear, if not respect.

"President Grant pulls a lot of strings, and I have to be selective in how I present certain facts." added the mogul.

Custer was on guard, he knew an important challenge was being issued here. Suddenly an attractive hostess offered the two men libations. Bennet accepted one of the proffered drinks, and he needed it; he was running the greatest risk of his life right now.

"This is a fine drink, General. Sip it sparingly, and the port will slowly permeate upward through the gin and will gently awaken the genever." James Bennet felt his stomach turn to ice as he felt the general's eyes searching him out. Custer was a teetotaler-did not drink, did not smoke.

"Be at ease, James, my man!" Custer was smiling and came off less wooden now, having seen the realization on the face of the press icon of his error in words.

"Of course Sir, my apologies, I had heard that you did not partake but it had slipped my mind during the course of our conversation." Bennett responded.

Bennet sipped and felt his blood warm. Possibly, he thought, an opiate had been added to the beverage. The opiated alcohol seemed to make the room float as the mogul found himself studying the man before him. The General or Colonel or whatever rank he was, thought Bennet, dominated the scene. Women and men alike sought to introduce themselves and heap praise upon him for his legendary exploits. The natural magnetism of his personality was obvious to everyone present. He cut a fine figure in his Union double breasted frock coat. The coat was eye catching; dark navy blue with cavalry collar bars and two sets of nine brass buttons that ran down both sides of the chest. Although wearing colonel epaulets on the shoulders, he wore the boldly colored golden sash of a general about his waist. His likewise golden hair cascaded to his shoulders in ringlets.

Not out of character, Bennet pressed the general with a personal question. "But you have not always abstained, is that not so?"

Custer did not seem to hear the question, although Bennet knew that he had.

"None of them ever led from the front, none of them ever took a bullet or played the odds like I do. Listen, Bennet..." Custer placed his arm over the shoulder of the newspaper magnate as they meandered through the throng of revelers.

"Do you know what I want to do most when I am President? Well, I'm going to let you in on a little secret."

Bennet held his shock in abeyance at the General's statement of bold intention, to bring the Army of the Potomac back up to full strength, and resurrect the armies of the Confederacy.

"Then," Custer continued as Bennet listened in mute astonishment, "I will invade Mexico and finish the job that we abandoned half completed in 1848."

The earlier question concerning the partaking of libations had indeed not been missed by the general. Indeed he had been a heavy drinker, and heavy drinking had led to heavy carousing. And much of that heavy carousing occurred as a West Point Cadet, when he was always at or near the bottom of his class. Just a hair's breadth from dismissal. Heavy drinking and carousing that often led to the brothel where his favorite paramour waited for him.

She was a stunning raven haired beauty from one of the Eastern tribes. A Mohawk, whose charms the drunken cadet could not resist. And those charms would linger, and linger, in the form of a painful and disgusting venereal disease known as the "clap." Most of the cadets suffered from it and often overcame it in time through the body's ability to combat the invasive bacteria. They would laughingly slap or "clap" a new recipient of the disease on his back as a form of comradery and male bonding.

Bennet accepted another drink from a proffered tray of shot glasses.

"Well!" Bennet expostulated. "That's the best way I can think of to reunite the United States! To get rid of this bitter divisiveness that lingers even ten years after the War."

Custer warmed to the magnate's frank collusion with his ambition.

"Then, after what I see as a two year campaign in Mexico, we can turn our eyes toward Canada, and unite the whole continent under the Stars and Stripes." added Custer.

As the opiated alcohol loosened the constraints of the newspaper man's thought process, he began to consider to himself how to invest his vast personal fortune, and who to allow in on the opportunity of a lifetime. There were new friends to be made, new business opportunities to be exploited with this priceless insider's knowledge.

Audie neither smoked nor drank; a promise he made to his future wife Libbie, during the years he tried to shake off the disease through exercise and clean living. But he never could shake it off-not completely. It would come and go. Sometimes it ravaged him so badly that he was nearly incapacitated. During a time he thought it was gone, he saw his longtime lover and first cousin, Mollie and infected her. She would not know for a long time, but by then it was too late. He had married Libbie, and infected her as well.

All this, I have wrought on these poor women, the females most dear to me. All in the course of drinking. He thought to himself. The Boy General had more on his mind than the clap, though.

Custer needed a victory in the field against the Sioux and Cheyenne, and a sycophantic press to publicize it. Out West, on the frontier, lay the last remaining chance to practice his Warrior's Ritual; and Bennet, seeing himself as a potential king maker, would assign his best ink man in the region, Clement A. Lounsberry to ride with the 7th. Lounsberry had, along with a junior editorialist named Mark Kellogg, founded the highly respectable Bismarck Tribune, which served the entire area of the Dakota Territories.

As with the other jewels that adorned his crown of achievements, James Gordon Bennet had his tentacles in the Bismarck Tribune as well. He would see to it that his enterprise would be the first to herald the account of the stunning victory of America's favorite icon, and be the only newspaper on the planet to have an actual reporter on the spot to give accounts in incredible detail, describing Custer, the man, the legend, the hero-and the next President of the United States of America! He, James Gordon Bennet, would make Custer the greatest publicity draw the world had ever known, and not only would sales of his newspapers soar, so would Custer's political debt to him.

« Chapter Four »

THE NEXT DAY FOUND Reno ranging ahead with a small entourage of hand-picked scouts. He took notes and carefully scrutinized the terrain that lay ahead. He did so in part because of the implied threat from Custer the evening before. He would do whatever his commanding officer ordered, out of respect, duty, and fear. He was not a well man, and the Army was all that he had at this stage in his life.

Major Reno was a trustworthy and capable career officer in whose charge General Terry placed the reconnoitering of this unexplored land of rolling hills, plains, valleys and rivers. Terry was in overall command of the three pronged offensive designed to crush Sioux resistance, and the decision to place Reno in charge of the initial reconnaissance had met with bitter resistance from Custer.

The matter of who was to lead the reconnaissance had been debated earlier, while on the Far West, a fast, powerful stern wheel steamboat that was transporting the 7th up the Yellowstone River.

"You've got enough on your plate already, George." placated the maneuvering Terry, as he tried to control the strong willed commander of cavalry.

"You're burning the candle on both ends, look..." Terry lowered his voice conspiratorially as if others were in the room, which was not the case. "...look, Grant has expressly forbidden you from bringing an AP correspondent on this expedition. I can make that all change, with the stroke of a pen." the general assured Custer, who could not remain still.

Custer was pacing back and forth in the wardroom of the Far West-a river boat steamer that served as command center for the far flung military expedition. It was a cutting edge shallow draft river steamboat launched in 1870, and piloted by the legendary Captain Grant Marsh. The Far West had set numerous speed records and had the ability to crawl over sandbars by use of steam capstans and spars. Although she was 190 feet in length with a beam of 33 feet, she only drew 30 inches of water when fully loaded with 200 tons of cargo. A triple decker, the low slung leviathan had two smoke stacks and a powerful pair of high pressure Herbertson steam engines with 15 inch pistons and a five foot power stroke. These were driven by steam generated by three boilers which turned the enormous single stern wheel, which measured 30 feet.

"Look." reiterated Terry, who easily controlled the psychotic officer, and enjoyed doing it. "Sit down, all your pacing is getting on my nerves."

Custer sat on the plush over padded leather club chair and locked eyes with his superior officer. "In return for what?" asked Custer.

Terry leaned back in the swivel chair behind his mahogany desk, locking his fingers behind his head, as he carefully made his gambit. He did not seem to notice the thud, then the rise and dip of the steamboat as it slammed into, and rode over a submerged sandbar.

"I'll come straight to the point, George. I'm nearing retirement. I'm ready to hang up the sword and shield and move on to the next chapter of my life, just as you are. I'll sign the waiver allowing a press correspondent to accompany you, in return for an ambassadorship to Spain. But I can't have the next President of the United States needlessly getting himself killed on a reconnaissance mission that a capable junior officer can carry out."

Custer seemed to unwind and relax, saying; "Alright, then. We've got a deal. What is it with you and Spain anyhow?"

But Custer's thoughts were on the topography of the land-largely uncharted that lay before him; land that was gouged by rivers of which the depths varied widely from one stretch to the next. What lay out there Custer largely only surmised based on rumor and hearsay. What little he knew for fact troubled him.

Oddly, these rivers ran north, and roughly parallel to one another in their meanderings. They were the Powder, the Tongue, and the Big Horn. They disgorged their contents into the Yellowstone River. There were a number of tributaries which supplied these water courses, one being of which was the aptly named Little Bighorn, which gave to the Big Horn River. The Little Bighorn had its origins in the extreme upper edge of Wyoming, where it began on the north face of the Bighorn Mountains and followed a bow like trajectory for 138 miles deep into Montana; it was fed by several tributaries of its own along the way.

Already, the Far West had traversed several rapids and many sandbars in its journey into the unknown. The central cabin where they sat was small, but lavishly furnished. Passenger accommodations were limited, and the steamer lacked a Texas deck, affording it a low profile with decreased wind resistance.

"I took a second major in addition to the mundane law degree I acquired at Yale. I found Spanish to be an interesting hobby, and have continued studying it during my leisure time." answered General Terry.

Custer was brought back to the present, and studied the man sitting before him, really for the first time. A general, he thought, fluent in Spanish.

"Would you consider a military governorship of Mexico, if that country were to seek our assistance in liberation?" inquired Custer.

Terry cut an unimposing image of a military man; slight of build, of medium height, his receding hairline remained stubbornly thick in the center, and the dark hair was combed over to the left side. This hair remained ungrayed, despite his years, and crowned a high forehead, wide at the top. This forehead Custer knew contained a brain of tremendous administrative and logistical talent. The sloe eyes were dark, overly large, and sparkled with intelligence. The face was narrow, lending to a false impression of weakness and lack of stamina. The full beard did little to dispel this image. Terry was evasive and noncommittal in his response.

"I have a substantial estate between Madrid and Merida that I acquired during the settlement of an egregious debt for a plaintiff during the time I was a lawyer." responded Terry, clearly caught off guard. "At this stage of my life a military governorship of Mexico would be, shall we say, worth considering?" General Terry added ambiguously, as if he were uncertain as to whether or not to make such a major course correction in the penumbra of his life.

Custer's gaze bore into Terry's eyes with an intensity that was unsettling. There was that slight shifting of the eyes from side to side, noticed Terry, as Custer tried to enter his mind.

"It would be worth a man's soul, wouldn't you say, Alfred?" said Custer, innocuously. Purposefully Custer began addressing his superior officer by his first name. Terry seemed not to notice the transgression, although Custer knew that he had.

« Chapter Five »

MAJOR RENO WITH HIS scouting expedition had the advantage of Cree scouts who were familiar with the area, and were scouting along the more distant Rosebud Creek. In the past, the Arikawa (Cree) had been semi nomadic, following the herds of buffalo but also growing fields of corn. During times of good harvest they would remain stationary, living in earth lodges; dome shaped dwellings constructed of bent saplings overlaid with wattle and daub, then covered with earth.

However, the influx of European settlers had obliterated their numbers with the introduction of small pox. Hard pressed and outnumbered by the Sioux, they became allies of the US Army and provided the bulk of the scouts in Custer's command. Alarmed by an Indian trail of gigantic proportions-the likes of which they had never seen before, the scouts urged Reno to advance the column and ride forth with them to see the trail for himself.

"This is an Indian trail of a magnitude most disproportionate to any I have yet beheld." opined a visibly concerned Major Reno. He turned around, telling his sergeant to rest the troops.

"Dismount! Prepare your meals, rest the horses, and make no fires." the sergeant shouted, the order was passed back down along the column.

Taking time to relieve himself–an act of nature he dreaded, Major Reno wiped his hands on his dust covered trousers. Having been diagnosed with syphilis many years before, he counted his lucky stars that it had not entered the tertiary stage. Sometimes it never did, the post surgeon had explained to him. But the act of micturition ignited a fire along the entire length of his urethra that sometimes made him scream. The oozing, purulent discharge from the urinary meatus of his penis was a constant annoyance, causing him to wear a padding to absorb the discharge and avoid embarrassment.

Looking through beady, rat-like eyes set behind a pudgy face, Reno assessed the cyclopean trail in troubled silence. Some parts of the Indian trail were gouged into ruts sixteen inches deep, filled with a talcum like dust. This trail led up the Rosebud Creek, between the Tongue and Bighorn Rivers. The Rosebud is a large creek, spilling from the Beartooth Mountains; it is roiled with white water rapids before it slows to a sluggish drunken meander, its banks lined with huge orange tiger lilies and other wild flowers.

The midday heat was sweltering and the biting buffalo gnats plagued the eyes of the horses and the dust covered troopers that swatted at them, causing clouds of dust to fly from their sleeves. The assault of deerflies on the horses was unrelenting. The Indian trail was titanic in its proportions, and another joined it, further on. Reno continued to survey the trail, which carried ominous portent.

The tails of the horses were giant fly swats that struck forcefully at the blood sucking horseflies that pestered their flanks. The horseflies could not be deterred, coming back again and again. Often alighting on soldiers and inflicting painful blood seeping bites. Most of the men wore light colored straw hats over closely cropped hair. Their hair was cut short to lessen the intolerable heat of the march, and the straw hats were more practical than the broiling felt cavalry hats. When in the field, discipline was lax as far as pettifogging went.

"In the field," Reno had heard Custer say, "We don't play games. We play for real."

Middle aged and widowed, Reno worried for a moment about how he would remarry-how he could hide the syphilis. Large sores on his penis that never healed oozed puss. The searing treatments of silver nitrate injected with a glass syringe directly into the urethra had not staunched the disgusting, fetid discharges. These thoughts passed in a couple of seconds as he walked alone a short distance up the Indian trail.

His shirt tugged tightly against the scarlet papules and nodules that scored his back in numerous wheals as he knelt down. Leaning forward, he scooped up a palm full of tan, talcum fine dust with his swollen hand- the palm of which was covered always in a rash, and let it escape in streams between the inflamed knuckles of his fingers.

"This is for real!" he said aloud to no one in particular. "Bloody Knife, what make you of this?" queried Reno.

The Indian trail resembled a huge deeply plowed field; having been furrowed by thousands of lodge polls pulled by the Indian ponies. Reno remembered his courses in mythology at West Point, regarding the Labors of Hercules when the demi-god plowed with the Cretan Bull. The absence of grass was a consternation; having been clipped to the ground by the enormous herds of Indian ponies, leaving nothing for the exhausted cavalry horses and pack mules. The bare expanse was littered with countless horse droppings, numbering in the hundreds of thousands.

"Big Indian village, plenty heap big, more warrior than Custer have bullets." was the Arikawa's reply.

Bloody Knife was not wholly Arikawa, being born of an Arikawa mother and a Hunkpapa Sioux father. As a boy he had been ostracized and viciously bullied by the Sioux, who considered him an inferior. Two of his brothers had been killed and scalped by the

Sioux, who left their bodies in the field to be eaten by wolves. Bloody Knife had a deep dislike of the Sioux, of Sitting Bull and of a particular man who had tormented him viciously-Gall.

"Too many injun to fight!" Spitting a long brown stream of tobacco juice, Bloody Knife added, "Maybe good we go back, tell Custer!"

"Too many to fight?" Custer studied the enigmatic face of his best scout and close personal friend, Bloody Knife.

"I was telling you," interjected Major Reno, "that the Indian trail I observed could only have been made by contingents numbering in the tens of thousands."

A pause of several moments ensued, which seemed like minutes to Reno. Custer was sitting on a stool behind the table on which lay a map-a map which grew in detail based on the reports of scouts as they provided new information on the topography that lay ahead. He was rubbing the temples of his forehead, his eyes were closed.

"How many?" Custer asked, without looking up.

"Tens of thousands, twenty thousand on this trail alone, by the looks of it. Give or take, but my estimate can't be far off." replied Reno, who fidgeted while Bloody Knife remained stoic.

"Go ahead and sit down, take a load off. What I mean is, how many days ride are they ahead of us?" clarified Custer.

Custer looked up at Bloody Knife, who remained standing.

"Two day, hard ride." ejaculated the stalwart Indian.

Reno took a sip of whiskey from the flask he always carried, adding; "General, we need to slow up and wait for the other columns to get here, we're way too far ahead of them, and there aren't enough of us to take them on alone."

"More injun than soldier have bullets." reiterated Bloody Knife.

Custer stood up and walked to the opening of the tent and stood there, looking out at the activity of the camp.

Pompous fool, thought Reno, *he's going to do it, he's going to go after the whole multitude of them by himself and get us all killed.*

Custer remained silent, alone in his thoughts.

"Martini!" shouted Custer.

Martini stood at attention listening to his commanding officer, who did not ever seem to notice he was even a human being. Custer seldom, if ever, gave scant thought to Martini. He was vaguely aware that the bugler was an Italian immigrant, one of many immigrants that had been dumped on the 7th. But like so many higher ranking officers, he paid little attention to those men who ranked far below him in the Army's social caste structure.

"Go find Lt. Varnum. Tell him to come here, now." the Yellow Hair ordered Martini, who looked back over his shoulder into the tent as he departed.

The general seemed to have already forgotten about Martini, and had sat down heavily on his field chair, leaning into the back of it. His head was facing the top of the tent and his eyes were closed, his officers talked among themselves as the general took no notice of them, either.

After Lt. Varnum arrived Custer stood up and faced Reno saying, "Varnum is going to take his scouts and leave here at 2200, after they've rested their horses and fed. I want them several hours ahead of us before we break camp."

Reno took another swig of whiskey in front of the General, who never drank but paid no mind. Alcoholism was rampant among the officers as well as the enlisted.

"Have the officers roust the men at 0300, we step off at oh five hundred." added the General.

Reno stood up, nervously knocking dust from his trousers before coming to attention.

"Yes Sir! Is that all, Sir?" asked Major Reno.

"That's all, Marcus. Carry on." Custer was surprised by Reno's competency and was pleased.

He turned and spoke to Bloody Knife who watched him with a wooden expression.

"Sit down, old friend. Now, talk to me openly." said Custer with the relaxed personal demeanor that he only shared with Bloody Knife.

« Chapter Six »

THEY HAD BEEN ON the march since before the light of day on the morning of the 23rd, moving up the Rosebud with the best scouts ranging far in the advance. The scouting party had stolen out hours earlier in the gloomy darkness, guiding through gulches and past towering hills into the quietness that presages the coming of dawn. Guiding not only through the ghostly gulches and past the towering hills that appeared as gossamer shapes in the purple gloom, but they had also long since guided beyond the furthest advance of Major Reno's scouting of the Indian trail. They could only discern the trail in the oppressive darkness when the horses stepped into the deep ruts, gouged into the hard earth, causing the horses to stumble. Often, the riders were thrown from their mounts or crushed beneath the heavy, grain fed horses.

"Get out there as far as you can ahead of us," Custer had told Lt Varnum, "when you locate the main encampment, secure a vantage point and send a pair of scouts back to me. Stay put and I'll bring up the main body."

Lt Varnum had ambitions of his own recalling an earlier conversation with the general in which the future of the lieutenant had been intimated.

"You find that encampment and lead me to it, Lieutenant Varnum, and I will make you a general!" promised the future President.

Custer was at the head of his mounted column of six hundred plus cavalrymen-soldiers in subdued grey and blue flannel shirts. The heavy wool regulation shirts were rolled into a bundle and secured onto the rear of the saddle, or placed into the saddle bags. They would be worn later in the afternoon, when the heat of the day subsided and the cool of the night set in.

The swallow tailed guidons were snapping in the breeze above the soldiers' sweat ringed straw hats. The guidon in the lead element had the distinctive triangle cut out of the fly, giving it the swallow tailed bird image. It was divided into two colors consisting of horizontal red and white stripes. In the upper left corner of the guidon was a blue overlay containing two concentric circles of stars, each representing an individual state in the Union.

Many of the straw hats were pinned up on the right side to facilitate aim with the Springfield carbines that were slung across their saddles in leather scabbards. All of the officers carried .45 caliber Colt revolvers at their side, as did many of the enlisted–purchased individually in not a few instances. The flower of US Army strength–the 7th Cavalry followed this trail relentlessly.

One of the officers, an Irishman, carried an eccentric walking cane with a silver handle in the shape of a wolf's head. He sat mounted atop his sorrel gelding while the flying column had stopped to water their horses. The captain of company I was an Irishman with a short temper, he grasped his walking cane and the reigns of his horse fiercely with his left hand as he rubbed his temples with his right. The foul tempered captain suffered bouts of insanity as his advanced syphilis entered the tertiary stage. His most capable sergeant approached him as the horses watered.

"Captain Keogh, Sir!" the sergeant addressed the tousle headed Irishman, "My men implore me to beseech you to ask the general for a longer break."

"Ride or die!" snarled the big Irishman, his green eyes narrowing into slits.

"But Sir!" expostulated the sergeant, who was slapped viciously across the mouth, drawing blood.

"You and many others carry the bruises of my cane on your backs! Make me look bad in front of the general and I'll see that you carry many more! Now, get out of here!" shouted the big captain in his Irish brogue.

"One of these days," threatened the sergeant, with hatred beaming from his eyes, "I will kill you. Go to the general, go ahead, go to him like a cry baby and report me. There is no one privy to this conversation but you and I, and I mean to kill you!"

The volatile captain stood up in his stirrups and swung the cane, hitting the sergeant across the side of the face.

"Is that all you've got? You fucking Mick!" challenged the sergeant, who grabbed the cane with his left hand, stopping another blow in mid stroke as the order was shouted to mount up and resume march.

"You're too big for your britches, Sergeant. Make your threats, I will see that you are horsewhipped and reduced in rank to private!" screamed the captain, the veins standing out on his neck and his face turning purple with rage.

"We're not in Europe, Captain." replied the sergeant, wiping the blood from his split lips with the back of his forearm, "I don't care what type of a family you're from. You're dead meat, mother fucker!"

As the day wore on, the sun climbed high into the Montana sky, and the dust covered column began to stretch out–stragglers falling behind. But the former general pressed them hard, continuing the march up the Indian trail which Major Reno had described in great detail.

Bloody Knife–Custer's best scout tried in vain to dissuade Lieutenant Colonel Custer from the object of his passion–the great Indian village which they knew awaited. The pair rode 50 yards ahead of the main body. "Can't win this one. Not enough soldier."

Custer continued to look far ahead, looking from left to right as he responded with a cliché. "The Sioux won't fight. They'll run at the first sign of us." Custer made the statement in such a way as to belie the unease he felt.

"You want to be the chief of the Bureau of Indian Affairs, well if Crook and Terry are in on this, it will diminish my achievement. Terry has confidence in me and that's why he let me go it alone." resumed Custer, who continued scanning the countryside straight ahead, and to either side of him as he spoke.

"Hmmmph!" grunted Bloody Knife, who didn't catch a word Custer had said.

The sound of the horse's feet and the din of the march added to the difficulty of understanding what the Yellow Hair had said. Besides, Bloody Knife knew, The Yellow Hair often spoke simply to hear himself speak. In this manner he would always have an agreeable audience.

The column became engulfed in a cloud of alkaline dust from the Indian trail. Some of the soldiers blew their noses into handkerchiefs, but not many. Most blew their noses with their fingers, and nearly all wore brightly colored bandanas over their faces to staunch the respiration of dust. The riders in the center and further back had it the worst. Their eyes were caked with dust and the granules acted like abrasive sandpaper when they open and closed the eyelids. At times some rode with their eyes closed, trusting their mounts to follow those in front of them.

So it was that the Boy General had issued the orders to halt, refraining from a bugle call.

"Let's unass right here and get the tent set up!"

Bloody Knife knew well the General's love of camping and his peculiar fondness for an overlarge tent which he had carried everywhere he went. Orders were passed to the rear with instructions for troop commanders to come forward to the command tent in an hour's time. It was a Sibley tent, a large conical canvas affair standing about twelve feet tall and shaped like a tepee. About eighteen feet in diameter at the base, it could shelter a dozen men and was supported by a center telescopic pole. It was staked to the ground and didn't require the use of guidelines; the tent was beige in color.

"General Custer, Sir!" the expostulation was in heavy Irish brogue.

"What do you need, Miles?" asked the Yellow Hair, perturbed at being interrupted in setting up his tent. "I said we'd hold a briefing in an hour."

"It's one of my sergeants, Sir. He threatened me! He threatened to kill me!"

Custer had been kneeling down, hammering the tent stakes into the ground prior to erecting the telescopic tent pole, but now he stood up, clearly annoyed. He faced the hulking Irishman with the boyish good looks and jet black hair. A foreigner,

Custer felt, who had no business being an officer in the Army.

"You son of a bitch!" yelled Custer, "If you cane one of my men again, I'll personally ram that wolf's head handle up your ass! Send that sergeant here that threatened to kill you!" demanded the general, his voice softened as an idea came to him.

The sergeant and the captain stood before Custer, who was aware of ubiquitous stares amid the soldiers who made ready the camp. The Boy General was aware of how hard he had pushed his men, and that everyone needed a respite.

"Take your shirts off, the both of you!" ordered General Custer, who was sitting on a folding field chair, fanning himself with his hat.

The sergeant quickly stripped off his shirt while the captain looked stupidly at the sitting general.

"Now, fight!" shouted Custer, "Fight like the sons of bitches you are!"

General Custer allowed his men to watch the brawl between the sergeant and the captain, knowing that their spirits would be bolstered by the break in routine. He had exceeded the projected rate of march by setting his column into motion at a furious pace, locating the trail, and sticking to it tenaciously. It was fortunate to have the pack train with provisions for both men and horses. Heavily armed details escorted the exhausted mounts to the Rosebud to rehydrate while the rest of the command watched the sergeant and the captain fight. Individual companies could be discerned by their unique guidons; the swallow tailed pennants were divided horizontally into two solid colors. The top half was red, with a white number "7" sewn into it. The bottom half of the guidon was white in color, with the letter of its company sewn onto it in red coloring.

The sergeant was getting the better of the big Irishman as the fight drew on. Except for the lookouts posted on the surrounding hills, and the details seeing to the exhausted horses, most of the command was circled around the officer and NCO as they fought.

"I'll cane you to death!" shouted the captain, drawing a boot knife and advancing on the pugnacious sergeant.

"Oh, let's see about that, Mick!" retorted the sergeant, scooping up a handful of sand and throwing it full into his knife wielding opponent's face.

"My eyes! My eyes! I'm blind! I'm blind!" screamed Captain Keogh, "I'll spill your guts for that!" Keogh wielded the short bladed boot knife with his right hand, swiping viciously with it as he frantically tried to clear the sand from his eyes with his left.

The stench of hundreds of unwashed bodies surrounded the two combatants; the stench of bodies of men who drank stale beer carried by the supply wagons and from whiskey bottles made of brown, translucent glass, of men who shouted and goaded them on, and of men whose fists slammed into open palms as they sang choruses of obscene songs while the two men fought.

"Now! That's what I call entertainment!" guffawed the Boy General, slapping his knee hard as he leaned forward on his field chair, laughing.

With the passage of the day, came the chilling of the starry night, whose icy stars were not the only lights to be seen, myriad fireflies competed in the luminescent pageantry, owing to the fact that the General had forbade the ignition of campfires until morning. Lights could also be seen, many miles away by the sentries picketed atop high ground, sentries who stood vigil against the solemn, taciturn men who built the distant fires that glittered eerily in the distance.

The camp fires of the Indian village were so numerous that a glow seemed to expand from the village, its luminescence reaching like a hand thousands of feet into the dark chill of the Montanan atmosphere. The 7th had drawn nigh unto the enemy they knew, because the wind outraged their ears with the resonance of hundreds of pagan war drums. The resonance faded as the wind ebbed, and grew as the wind renewed. As darkness settled, the drumming became more distinct, and the shrill notes of war flutes could be heard above the timbre of the rolling drums.

« Chapter Seven »

GENERAL CUSTER SLEPT fitfully in the Sibley tent, a deep, exhausted sleep; resplendent in the imageries of scarlet nightmares. Often a variation of the same dream; it always began near the end, but never resolved. The dreams included characters from his past, which were out of the timeline in the dream, or the dream would take place out of context with the geography, but one element remained constant-the Indian. Always hunting or fleeing from Indians, this time through an endless ocean of prairie grass. Custer shifted in his sleep on the cot inside the tent, his sleep deepening, the nightmare growing in luxuriant detail and realism...

As he kneeled he rested the butt of his Spencer repeating rifle into the spongy, damp grass of the meadow and he leaned into the rifle for support, taking the strain off of his haunches. Underneath his buckskin jacket he wore a blue cavalry shirt, outside of which adorned a unique double shoulder holster from which depended two English Webley bulldog revolvers. A gun belt bearing a Colt .45 revolver cinched tightly around the buckskin jacket. There was apprehension in the blue eyes that searched the green open expanse that surrounded and flanked the Indian trail. The sky was blue, but there was no sun. Adrenaline dilated pupils bored into the endless beyond.

Rising, he began to slink cautiously along, having been for hours on the hunt. Trying to find the quarry was like trying to find a needle in a haystack in this green verdure of tall grass; aware the path hugged the margins of the Arkansas River, he stuck to it, like a revolver in a holster. He tried not to make noise as he padded carefully along, but he knew that a sound, no matter how small, would not escape the ears of the Indian.

He was alert, every sense on edge, he was listening with such intensity as he crept along that he could hear his ears ringing. The grasses were so dense, so suffocating that eyesight was relegated to a secondary level of importance. It was a sixth sense that made him freeze in place, crouching, rifle at the ready. He didn't breathe, he didn't move, he wondered what had made the noise, that was so faint, so subtle, he wondered if perhaps he had imagined it. There was not to be heard the chirp of birds, nor the high pitched whir of cicadas, the silence was deafening.

The dream oddly changed it's time and location, as dreams often do. He found himself in the dining room of the brother of his grandfather, who was reading aloud from the Bible to his wife; both were seated at the table.

"...and it says here, in the book of Matthew..." Custer's great uncle continued to read to his wife, not noticing his great nephew's appearance.

Custer stood before them, obediently at the table. He woke up, and then slid back into deep, uneasy slumber, into the part of the dream he favored.

But suddenly he was inexplicably somewhere else, he knew not where. It was earlier in the day and he was walking toward a single story clapboard house at the side of a roadway. The unpainted house stood alone, it was a solidly built frame house with a wide front porch. He had the impression it was a wayfarer's inn for outlanders, vagabonds, and ne'er do wells. Something about the place raised his level of awareness.

"Hello!" he shouted as he mounted the steps.

No response came from within the house; it came from under the building. He stepped back down and walked around to the side.

Kneeling down and peering underneath he could see that it was a pier and beam structure, he could see that a square shaped pit had been excavated about four feet deep, and there were four Caucasian women attired in dark Puritan dresses which had gone out of style 200 years before. Their hair was brown, and pulled back tightly. They did not wear hair covers. The dresses were dark brown and full length with white bib collars and soiled white aprons. The women were busy doing something with their hands at a darkly stained table made of heavy rough cut oak boards. They were speaking amongst one another. For the first time in one of his nightmares Custer felt fear.

"Hello?" said the General, his mouth was without saliva as he swallowed, his Adam's apple rising and falling. The women ignored him, although he knew they were aware of his presence. Suddenly from behind he felt a pressure on his back pushing him into the pit with the women.

"Confound it! What the devil! I've got to wake up! Wake up!"

He felt his stomach rise as though he were falling from a great height, and when he stopped falling, he was prostrate on the earthen floor of a tepee adorned with horrific symbols. He looked up into the fierce face of what appeared to be a Sioux Medicine man. The Sorcerer uttered a dialect he'd never heard before and then he looked into his eyes; dark eyes of obsidian that seemed to reach into his soul. He struggled against the power that was overwhelming his will to resist when suddenly he was awoken from the dream by a violent shaking of his shoulder.

"General, it's Reveille! Awaken!"

« Chapter Eight »

THE BEDROOM IN GENERAL Custer's two story home at Fort Abraham Lincoln was illuminated by half a dozen whale oil lamps which cast a warm glow across the lavishly furnished room.

"Make ready my bath!" came a command delivered by a female voice.

Elizabeth Custer told her maid servant, a strikingly beautiful Indian girl of about 20 years to prepare her bath as she began undressing. Elizabeth knew she would not be fully undressed before the raven haired beauty had filled the tub with scented, steaming water.

Libbie Custer, as those intimate with the Custer family knew her, was in her early thirties, and still the most beautiful of all the officers' wives stationed on the post of Fort Abraham Lincoln. As she stood in front of the mirror she unpinned her auburn colored hair, listening to the girl pouring another bucket of hot water into the Victorian styled bath tub. Although she always slept in a night gown when her husband was home, this was not so when she was alone. And the avoidance of nudity in her husband's presence was, to her, a proper reprisals for the affliction he had cursed her with. Yet she enjoyed the nudity she displayed occasionally in front of other officer's wives, more often in front of her sister in law, and especially in front of her Indian servant, who she could sense was made uncomfortable by it.

The black Victorian touring hat lay carelessly tossed on the bed, as Libbie let her hair fall down to her shoulders. She began unbuttoning the white and black pin striped high necked walking blouse, which was secured by five buttons, and pulling it off, she flung it haphazardly to the floor.

Too fast, she thought to herself, *what's the hurry? It's going to take that little imp another 30 minutes to get my bath ready!*

She had always enjoyed displaying herself in front of other women, especially in dormitories of the women's schools her father had sent her to. Off came the thin black velvet belt, followed by the pinstriped walking skirt and Edwardian hoop underskirt. Leaving the silken white underbus corset on for the moment. Libbie often did not wear drawers or tap pants underneath her dresses. She admired her beauty in the full length mirror-a gift from Alexis-the nephew of the Tsar of Russia.

"Et-nah-wah-ruchta! The tub must be but half full." she said, realizing too late she had shouted.

Anticipation of the next few moments was almost overwhelming.

"It's good enough as it is, Et-nah-wah-ruchta, you've done a very admirable service for me. Now, please come help me dispense with this corset."

Et-nah-wah-ruchta approached the wife of General Custer as she always did at this time; nonchalantly, in a matter of fact, orderly fashion-but inwardly she was very uncomfortable during these moments. To her stoicism was added the levity of her situation.

About the lamp lit room lifelike eyes gazed down from mounted trophies that adorned the papered walls.

"I'm going to my bath directly; bring more hot water as I mean to wash my hair as well." said Libbie Custer with the easy air of authority that came with a lifetime of ordering attendants to perform trivial tasks.

The tiny bathroom was located almost at the other end of the large house, sandwiched between the dining room and the kitchen. The bathroom door opened directly from the lengthy dining room and was directly opposite one of the two front doors. These two doors were almost side by side and admitted from the large veranda that swept the entire front of the two story home-a mix of Victorian and ranch architectures.

"Yes ma'am Mrs. Custer. I have the water heated beside the stove, eh? All very hot, oils, salts, and the soap." responded Et-nah-wah-ruchta, the favorite servant of Elizabeth Custer, who hoped to leave the Custer house early.

The fort commander's wife exited the bedroom ahead of Et-nah-wah-ruchta, who would continue beyond the bathroom and into the kitchen, where the large wood burning stove continually maintained the heat of two or more galvanized wash tubs of water. The maid servant saw the muscles play underneath the dimpled behind of Libbie Custer as she carelessly strode the length of the dining room completely naked.

The diminutive bathroom, the size of a master bedroom walk in closet, was illuminated by two wall mounted lanterns, which cast a soft yellow glow, and reflected off the glass of the large window, which began at knee level. The curtains were drawn open to allow cool air to enter through the window screen. The eyes of dozens of grass hoppers which lined the metal screen glowed eerily as they reflected the light of the two lanterns.

Et-nah-wah-ruchta kneeled beside the black, cast iron stove which sat atop fire bricks inlaid into the mahogany floor. Beside this were several galvanized tubs for maintaining hot water, and in one of these was a tin bucket filled with steaming water. Picking this up she poured an amount into a brown two gallon stone pitcher half filled with tepid water and tested it with her finger before taking it the short distance to where Libbie bathed.

The General's wife had already stepped into the hip bath-a small, high backed pewter tub contoured at the low end to allow for the legs to extend over and for the feet to rest on the floor. She had already lathered down with a fragrant soap made of sassafras root; she was facing Et-nah-wah-ruchta as she entered the bathing room, bent at the waist washing the crease behind her knees. She was very shiny and slippery in appearance Et-nah-wah-ruchta thought, in the soft glow of the lamp light. Her small breasts swayed and jiggled as she rubbed her skin with a large sponge.

"Go ahead and wet my hair." the general's wife said to the servant, conscious of her nudity in front of the clothed woman.

Et-nah-wah-ruchta poured the hot, nearly steaming water onto the back of Libbie Custer's head, as Libbie worked her fingers in it to ensure saturation. After adding a shampoo, she thoroughly massaged her scalp, and used the shampoo from her soaked hair to clean her face.

"Rinse." she said authoritatively.

Squatting to a crouching position, she faced about and sat down fully in the small tub, legs extended over the contoured lips and feet on the floor.

"Fill it the rest of the way, now." directed Libbie, who was fully aware of the discomfort Et-nah-wah-ruchta felt in these moments.

Libbie was reclined back, arms on the rests that winged out on either side of the small tub, head resting on the high end of the tub, which canted back to allow for long periods of comfortable soakings. This was the part that Elizabeth anticipated the most, as Et-nah-wah-ruchta returned several more times with the water pitcher full of nearly steaming water. Elizabeth knew that she was in full view of her female servant-practically spread with nothing but bubbles to hide what was beneath. The hip bath tub was popular and left little to be hidden, as the water line would barely exceed the navel.

Libbie liked to talk to Et-nah-wah-ruchta while nude, knowing that her captive audience could not leave. She especially liked to speak to her while in the bathtub. The sense of awkwardness that Et-nah-wah-ruchta betrayed with evasive answers and jilted conversation served to excite Libbie. This reminded her of her days at boarding schools, when she paraded naked around the other girls every chance she got, and relished the way they tried to distance themselves as she spoke to them in the afterhours, brazenly naked in the female dormitory room.

"Et-nah-wah-ruchta, I was mortified to have been compelled to impose such a chore upon you, but to lie down in this tub but for a moment or two has brought to me today a discovery of sheer Heaven! Today was nothing but sheer fatigue, for I was perfectly robust, and I could laugh and talk with the wives of my husband's dear friends. Though I was nothing quiet equal to the task of sitting mounted on a horse nearly all day as we watched the dogs being set upon wild wolves!

"I principally feel exhausted from being in the saddle all day. Otherwise I would express contentment robustly for having been blessed to frequent such bucolic scenery as I enjoyed this morning and afternoon. The advantage provided by these pastoral settings cannot be over amplified. Why, disinclination, or even antipathy has less repugnance than a moribund existence back East. What an infecund existence that it would be, to endure a mundane presence in the security of a modern city, with nothing but the doldrums of book reading clubs and dreary vitriolic diatribes. Oh! You should have seen how my Audie's hounds ripped the throats from those unfortunate wolves!"

She used her elbows to adjust her position in the tub as she added emphasis. Et-nah-wah-ruchta heard the skin of Libbie's behind rub against the bottom as she slid herself up in the tub. It made a squeaking, rubbing sound.

"You could hear the bones snap as they crushed the wolves' legs with their jaws!"

Et-nah-wah-ruchta paused, shifting her straight, black, waist length hair behind her shoulders; she wore a knee length buckskin dress with nothing on underneath. She searched Libbie Custer with stygian, almond shaped eyes, not understanding most of what Libbie said, but comprehending the gist of the statements. In her high pitched, distorted English she attempted to converse with her matron, out of a loathing sort of pity, and also prudence.

Libbie discerned a cold cruelty in the nasal tones of the halting English.

"When two man want marry same woman, woman choose, or make fight. I make fight, I make 'em fight in water, I like watchin'."

There was no hint of a smile from the thin, cruel lips under the short, hooked nose.

"Help me up and towel me. How long did the fighting endure?" ejaculated Libbie, who did not particularly notice that she had spoken the words in an authoritative, commanding tone.

Libbie Custer had one foot planted on the floor and the other perched on the tub as she dried her leg, Et-nah-wah-ruchta toweled Libbie's back, while searching for words.

"Fight all day, husband have arm round other man neck, keep down in water, not let go, make spit out air. Dead man, he get throw on trash heap, for dogs to eat."

Libbie turned around and abruptly faced Et-nah-wah-ruchta, intentionally making her small pointed breasts jiggle with the halt of the motion. The unbrushed hair of Libbie Custer was wet, and the angelic face was set with gray blue eyes which were alive with merriment.

"So you made them fight to the death for you, and the stronger of your champions sent your other suitor on an irrevocable descent into Hades beneath the River Styx! Oh! If I could but be witness to such demonstrations of athletic ardor! Surely you will arrange me audience to such a marital contest of young champions!"

Added to Elizabeth Custer's fetish for exhibitionism was also a streak of voyeurism. Although this was less so, it was nevertheless a fact. Many times she had spied from her window at Et-nah-wah-ruchta bathing with her husband in the nearby creek, and would write about it in her diary.

"And what a handsome pair of excursionists you two make! I've watched you and your fine looking husband frolic in the creek as you bathed, and how you chased him with the towel! Now prepare my bed as I finish up in here, dear friend."

Et-nah-wah-ruchta was of the Cree nation, which was held in contempt by the Sioux-primarily for their long standing practice of incest. Libbie also knew that the two contenders for the Indian maiden's breasts were her brothers-twins, a rarity among the Native American tribes.

The sheets were pulled back on the bed as Et-nah-wah-ruchta prepared the final steps in the ritual before leaving the Custer home; this always involved removing the sleeping gown of the General's wife, although she was clueless as to why her matron even bothered to don the apparel while the General was gone.

"Help me off with my gown, and then brush my hair." instructed Libbie, who then sat a chair facing the French dresser, or commode, as it was known.

The commode was a popular feature in the bedrooms of officer's wives and had a prominent mirror attached, into which a lady would look as she sat and brushed her hair. Libbie looked into her reflection as Et-nah-wah-ruchta brushed the tangles from her shoulder length hair. The brush would catch on a tangle, causing the general's wife to cry out in exasperation, exaggerating the discomfort inflicted. She did this to further frighten her maid servant.

"You sadistic little sprite! You're trying to pull out all of my hair!" spat the general's wife, who exaggerated her discomfort and tried to intimidate the servant.

Standing suddenly, Libbie slid the chair backward into Et-nah-wah-ruchta, causing her to grunt. Libbie then looked down at her clothing which lay askew on the floor.

"I saw you looking at my corset. You may have it." said Libbie, although the offer was not stated as obligatory, it really was.

Et-nah-wah-ruchta was surprised and always tried to appear gracious in the denial of gifts. She did not want to deepen her indebtedness any further to her matron than it already was. Et-nah-wah-ruchta and her husband lived like a queen and a king compared to the other members of the Cree. Elizabeth had showered her Indian servant with trivial, throw away type items of décor and utility. While these items were taken for granted by the officer's wives, these same items were coveted by the impoverished aboriginals. Cooking utensils, clothing, heavy winter blankets, just to name a few items, Elizabeth showered gifts onto her captive audience. The tepee of Et-nah-wah-ruchta was furnished like a palace compared to the other tepees of the tribe.

"Mrs. Custer-I cannot, I am not thin woman as you, not gonna fit me." expostulated the Indian servant, who secretly coveted the undergarment.

Libbie Custer walked across the floor, barefoot, and lay atop the bed, felinely, and sprawled herself belly down on the buffalo fur coat that served as a comforter, this buffalo was very rare in the Dakotas, her husband having shot it from the only known herd in the territory. Propping her chin on her hands, smiling, she responded to her servant.

"Well, I want to see it on you! I can only imagine the passion that such apparel will inspire in your champion!"

The native's erector pili muscles contracted, causing the fine hairs on her arms to rise in adrenaline fueled alarm, Et-nah-wah-ruchta reiterated that she could not fit into the tightly fitting Victorian underclothing peculiar to white women, and that her husband was impatient for her return.

"Not gonna fit, Mrs. Libbie. Injun woman not like white woman. I too big, big tummy." parried Et-nah-wah-ruchta, who was horrified at the prospect of appearing naked in front of the strange white woman.

"Too nice to give to Injun woman, can't put on white woman clothes. Not gonna fit!"

"Try it on, I'll tighten the laces for you." answered Libbie Custer who was still smiling, but there was an edge in her voice...

« Chapter Nine »

LT. VARNUM REACHED the Crow's Nest perched high on the divide, and could see 15 miles to the Little Bighorn. The river appeared as a tiny snake, bending and winding its way through the topography, made hazy by the distance. The Crow's Nest was a high promontory located in the diminutive Wolf Mountains. What he saw astonished him; there on the side of a prominent hill was a seething, eddying mass of horses the likes of which he had never seen. He would have missed it had not his Indian scouts kept pointing it out to him. The hillside was blanketed with Indian ponies, the ocean of semi-wild, short, stout ponies seemed to roil and convolute, changing shape like a gigantic multi-celled organism as it foraged.

Lt. Charles Albert Varnum was the commander of Custer's scouts in the Little Big Horn expedition. The son of a Civil War major, he graduated seventeenth out of fifty seven at West Point's class of 1872. Like most cavalrymen, he was lean set; his brown hair was cut short, and receded suddenly along both temples, leaving a thick, but narrow widow's peak common to many of the soldiers. Below his unnaturally high forehead, reptilian eyes scintillated through primitive binoculars at the massive herd of Indian ponies. These binoculars were extremely limited in their magnification capabilities.

"Send for the General, forthwith!" hissed Varnum through clenched teeth.

Varnum lowered the binos and looked directly at Bloody Knife. Bloody Knife hustled from the piranha faced lieutenant.

Blue eyes peered through the Lemaire binoculars; the mainstay of the Army since the Civil War, they were of the narrow focus Galilean style, really the best of the opera types using the convex objective and concave eye piece lenses. Their magnification power was rudimentary at distance.

"I don't see anything." stated General Custer, as he scanned the horrifying spectacle laid out fifteen miles away.

Inwardly his adrenal cortex glands were secreting volumes of the hormone as he beheld a herd of Indian ponies numbering in excess of 20,000. He could see the end portion of a village that was a half a mile wide and four miles long. His heart was pounding with excitement-and worry-that the Indians might escape.

To belay the fear that his scouts betrayed, he reiterated loudly enough so that the contingent could hear his words.

"I don't see anything, but we'll have a little pow wow, discuss this thing and get after it." said the Boy General, who placed the binoculars back into their leather case fumbling as he did so with over tensed nerves.

The Yellow Hair looked over to Lt. Cooke, and issued a curt order. "Head back to Reno's command, find that piece of shit Lt. DeRudio. Tell that Italian son of a bitch I need his binoculars. Now move!"

Custer had looked through DeRudio's binoculars on numerous occasions and coveted them. The Boy General had hinted that the Lt. should give them to him as a gift, and that he would consider it a personal favor, but DeRudio had refused. In reprisal, Custer had used his rank and placed another officer in command of DeRudio's company, assigning him instead to a subordinate position under Major Reno. DeRudio bristled at the retribution.

"No! I will not relinquish my field glasses! There are not another pair like these on the continent of North America!" the flustered Lt. DeRudio retorted angrily to Lt. Cooke.

The officer's accent betrayed his Italian ethnicity. DeRudio knew, too, that his life could depend on the telescopic binocular vision, the pristine clarity and amazing magnification inherent in the revolutionary new design of these optics.

"What the hell is going on here!" demanded Major Reno, approaching on horseback.

"The General wishes that I give to him my field glasses, there are no others like these!" complained DeRudio to Reno.

The new design was a quantum leap over what was currently in use. Employing Keplerian optics, in which the image is viewed through oculars, and accompanied with diopter focus rings to zoom in and focus the image. These innovations made DeRudio's binoculars the first truly modern field glasses in the United States. Incorporated as well were Porro prisms, to correct the upside down imagery that occurred. These binoculars were a special gift to the Italian by the renowned European optician Ignazio Porro.

"Just give Lt. Cooke the glasses, I know you're chaffed at having your company taken from you, but the General remembers favors, and it might get you your company back." suggested Major Reno in a placating manner.

"No, no sir! We need these optics here! Our lives depend on them!" retorted DeRudio, his voice carried with it an arrogance that outraged the ears of Major Reno.

"Lt. Cooke, if Lt. DeRudio does not relinquish his binoculars to you forthwith, shoot him!"

Quickly DeRudio unslung the black leather binocular case from his shoulder and knocked his hat off in doing so. Dismounting, he handed the Porros over to Lt. Cooke and kneeled to pick up his straw hat, and donning it looked up to see the rear of Cooke's horse as he prepared to return to Custer at once. It was at that moment that a powerful stream of urine issued from the horse's rear, hitting DeRudio squarely in the face and knocking his hat off again.

« Chapter Ten »

AT THE HEADWATERS OF Ash Creek, which gave to the nearby river, Custer had returned to his command as they watered their mounts, and he attended to personal matters. Mark Kellogg had ridden up beside the General and took shorthand notes of Custer's actions as he spoke of the day's progress with confidants. Then the General stopped talking for a moment, and seemed to take Kellogg in on a one to one basis for the first time.

"Mark, this is the most important story you have ever done in your life up until now. That's not only history that you're writing on that notepad, you're also making the future possible. How would you like," Custer leaned toward Kellogg, "to be the White House Press Secretary? It's a key cabinet position that I've been thinking about creating."

Kellogg's rapid fire pencil strokes stopped in midsentence as he digested the import of the offer Custer was making, and grasped the importance it meant not only to the historical perspective and press acclaim, but to his personal future as well. Kellogg dismounted and walked back to the headquarters section, thinking to himself.

Kellogg was here purely by chance; it was his boss, Clement Lounsberry who by virtue of his senior authority and personal ambition should have been the one taking notes and being addressed by the next President of the United States. Lounsberry had founded the Bismarck Tribune and was prepared to go on the Custer expedition, having delegated the responsibilities of running the small daily newspaper to his capable assistant, Kellogg. Although small in circulation, the Tribune covered a huge geographical expanse. Marcus recalled the events subconsciously as he digested the import of what the general had offered him.

"Marcus, by all that is Righteous and Holy, I should be accompanying Custer on this crusade." Lounsberry had told Kellogg, there was regret in his voice and pain in his bloated face.

Kellogg listened to the morbidly obese Lounsberry with rapt attention as the boss of the Bismarck Tribune revealed the unexpected turn of events, of how a bullet fired a dozen years before was about to change his entire life.

"My leg is killing me! I haven't slept in days on account of the pain and there's no way I can ride with the Cavalry." complained Lounsberry, who rubbed the leg with both hands as it was propped on a stool while he sat in a swivel chair.

Kellogg knew Lounsberry was right; the former Civil War Colonel had taken a bullet in the leg at Spotsylvania which shattered the bone. It had never healed and the newspaper man had to walk with a cane, and sometimes crutches. The once active man had become fat and sedentary. He was bald on top, but combed his hair over it, making it merely appear to be thin.

Black, doll like eyes were set in a bloated face, and a grotesque dark walrus moustache overhung his upper and lower lips. Often there was food or nasal discharge embedded in the hairs. Lounsberry knew what he was giving up, but in a final gambit for fame and fortune he made his bid, placing his bet on his best man-Kellogg.

"You know, of course, what this opportunity means for you." stated Lounsberry.

Kellogg, who was too stunned to reply at once, remained silent. This was a once in a lifetime opportunity, he realized. A chance at the Holy Grail of journalism.

"I've appreciated all of the long hours you've put into the Tribune more than you know. This chance of a lifetime I'm giving you is in gratitude for your service." concluded Lounsberry, who fought to contain his tears, stoically.

When Kellogg answered, it was exactly what Lounsberry wanted to hear.

"Rest assured, Mr. Lounsberry, I always return a favor." responded the stunned Kellogg, who was almost speechless with disbelief.

Kellogg joined the enlisted men who were securing their regulation blue blouses onto the rear of their McClellan saddles. They were to be worn later in the cool of the evening. The Army had chosen the McClellan saddle not only because it was light and inexpensive but also because by its very design was conducive to the long, hard testicle busting rides of mounted warfare; the center of the saddle had been removed-leaving an empty space so that hard pounding did not bruise testicles. Attached to the D ring of the saddle was a carbine thimble-a leather socket that the Springfield slid into. The thimble provided a readier access for the Springfields than the leather scabbards that some troopers preferred when they neared their objective.

They were wearing the issue grey flannel undershirts and about their waists were privately purchased ammunition belts for the cartridges of their new Model 1873 Springfield carbines and the revolutionary equally new .45 caliber single action1872 Colt revolvers. Their blue cavalry trousers had white canvas reinforcing the posterior, from the knees up to the seat. The trouser cuffs were not tucked into the leather short topped boots. They were filthy, rough, veteran fighting men, dressed and equipped to do the job, not pass in review on parade. Six hundred and seventy five of them.

The troopers wasted not a moment in watering, feeding, and tending the horses. Many horses had festering blisters that had formed under the saddles. On the left shoulder of each horse was branded "US" and on the left hip was seared forever, "7."

The days of unrelenting hard riding had given Associated Press reporter Mark Kellogg blisters along the inside of his thighs which had burst. To these ulcerations he applied bear grease. His glasses were smeared with sweat that he carefully wiped off with a soft cloth, to avoid scratching the thick lenses with the gritty dust that adhered to them.

Kellogg walked painfully to where Custer's meeting was beginning to take place. Everything was moving fast. The General was standing near a knoll beside the creek issuing frag orders.

"Gentlemen," Custer said in his rapid fire high pitched voice, "They discovered our presence and at once their scouts hastened away to alert the entire encampment. Of course it is useless now to entertain the illusion of surprise, and our intention to cross the river in the morning is necessarily changed to immediately!"

Custer spoke rapidly, although his thought processes were even faster, thought Kellogg, who short-handed notes with pencil of everything that was said as Custer observed approvingly.

"A large village of Sioux and Cheyenne has been reported by Lt. Varnum and his scouts, even now he sent word that they attempt escape!" shouted Custer, whose right hand clenched into a fist and pumped up and down as he shouted, on his hands were the large gauntlets popular with the cavalry.

As Custer described the situation phase of the order, he wore a large, cream colored straw hat, a blue flannel shirt, his buckskin trousers were tucked into his high topped, 1872 US Cavalry issued boots.

"It will be possible perhaps for us to prevent the hostiles from effecting an escape. Lt. Varnum is directed to employ his scouts in watching and reporting their movements!" continued to shout the general, he was pacing back and forth as he spoke, while Martini was holding the reins of Vic, his horse.

The General was rapidly delivering the abbreviated order, and went hastily to the execution phase, sometimes starting his sentences over to compensate for the rapidity of his thoughts.

"Captain Benteen, you will take three companies; D, H and K, with the objective of screening to the south-east along our left, Captain McDougal I'm assigning you and company B the pack train! Major Reno, you will take your companies A, G and M and assault the village when we come upon it! I will reinforce you! Lt. Varnum, is to continue scouting ahead of the vanguard...I will entertain questions!"

Captain Benteen was the first to speak up. He was wearing the blue cavalry trousers with canvas insert and suspenders over the long sleeved flannel shirt held up the trousers. His sleeves were rolled up above the elbows and his wide brimmed straw hat was pushed back far on his head as he spoke.

"Hadn't we better keep the regiment together, General? If this is as big a camp as they say, we'll need every man we have." reasoned Benteen, who was wearing a non-regulation gun-slinger styled belt which held two Colt .45 revolvers.

Custer looked into the eyes of Benteen, cold, lifeless old doll eyes that resided behind eyelids nearly always wide open-the stare Custer had seen many times before in men who'd done too much killing.

"You have your orders." expostulated the commanding officer of the 7th Cavalry.

Captain Benteen had not underestimated the commanding officer's total hedonism. Custer had not even taken the question seriously, so self-absorbed was he in himself. The General was well aware of Benteen's dislike for him, but Benteen was no coward, and what he had to say, no matter how derogatory, he would say bluntly, face to face.

The Boy General had looked at the gargantuan encampment for nearly an hour using the binoculars of DeRudio, and was nearly overcome with joy and excitement. The desire to initiate the movement to contact was irresistible.

« Chapter Eleven »

MAJOR RENO CROSSED the Little Big Horn at a point where it was about 35 feet wide. If ever he were to cross his own Rubicon, it was here. When Reno launched his attack, it was at full gallop with a total of 134 officers and men in addition to 16 scouts. The distance to the village was about three miles over flat terrain that abutted the river. To Reno's flank was scrub and cottonwood. He had asked no questions when he was ordered to charge, and almost immediately he ran into problems.

Thousands of warriors swarmed out of the southern end of the village to meet him. Many were armed with repeating rifles which they would shoot as they ran, not taking aim but pointing in the general direction of the approaching cavalry. Others approached also, shooting arrows at a high trajectory, drawing back on the bowstrings and releasing the shafts as they walked.

Immediately Reno ordered a dismount, and as his command formed a skirmishing line, one of the soldier's horses bolted-with the trooper still on it-into the village. He was immediately taken to Sitting Bull, technically not a chief, but a religious Holy Man. To the Arikawa and soldiers who knew of him, he was a sorcerer; a High Priest of the darkest arts of black magic.

"Dismount! Dismount! Skirmishers quickly, on the double! One in four! To the trees! One in fours to the damned tree line and make it quick!" shouted the major who made no attempt to ensconce the panic betrayed by his voice.

One in four men ran with the horses to the wood line as the paltry remaining number fumbled with the trap doors of their Springfield carbines, loading one round at a time.

"Fire at will! Stop them!" screamed Major Reno.

Reno was running back and forth along the line, bent double at the waist to lessen his chances of being hit by the increasing volume of Indian fire.

"Faster! Faster! You've got to get those bullets down range and keep them going!" urged Reno, whose face and forehead were beaded with perspiration, his pupils dilated.

Some of the men held rounds in their mouths, and three between the fingers of their left hand to speed reloading as they shot the huge .45-55 one bullet at a time. Others fumbled with trembling hands and dropped bullets into the grass and desperately reached for the ammo belt as all hell broke loose. Sometimes the trap door closed before the soldier got another round into the breech.

"Dammit I've got to piss!" shouted Reno, the shout was absorbed like a sponge into the maelstrom of gunfire.

Reno lay on the ground to avoid being hit by the metal storm of gunfire while he tried to urinate. He fumbled with and unbuttoned his trousers and flung aside the syphilis drenched cloth he'd placed there to absorb the drainage. The urine was backed up behind a mucous plug that ran the entire length of his urethra. It was only the hydraulic pressure of his full bladder that dislodged the germ laden plug from the scarred, constricted urethra.

"Ahhhhhhhh!" the major screamed above the gun fire as the urine burned through his penis like a hot poker.

The din was deafening, Reno could hardly hear his own voice as he continued to scream above the melee. The act of micturition lasted a full two minutes, and by the time he was finished, he was screaming so hard that no sound issued from his mouth.

The Indians exploded from out of a shallow gorge to the direct front, a hundred yards distant. They were running and firing 16 shot 1860 Henry repeating rifles, thousands of them-while hundreds of warriors armed with Henrys and 13 round Winchester 1866 Yellowboy lever actions blasted through the wavering skirmish line and got in their rear. Shooting wildly, the Indians took a terrible toll.

"Bloody Knife! Where's Custer!?" Reno screamed at the top of his lungs as he buttoned his trousers.

Bloody Knife saw the major's lips moving but couldn't make out what he said as the gunfire drowned his voice. Desperately, Bloody Knife reloaded his Winchester-a personal gift from the Yellow Hair. As he slid the cartridges into the loading gate of the big repeater, a bullet whizzed by his face like a hornet, causing him to distance himself from the hysterical major.

"I go ask aroun' maybe find what's up with Boy General!" shouted Bloody Knife back to Reno.

Major Reno saw that the valley was filling with the smoke of burnt black gun powder, and a growing grass fire. The smoke was beginning to obscure the cyclopean sized village. The village was one half of a mile wide, extending for miles, until it vanished beneath a dip in the land, and reappeared, stretching as far as he could see.

"Damn my soul! Where is he!?" expostulated the exasperated Army major.

The troopers, many whose hats had been shot off, were reforming into clumps, some were prying at swollen spent cartridge casings, trying to extract them from the chamber with anything they had at hand. The chambers of the carbines were heating to such a point that sometimes the rounds would ignite upon insertion.

Several thousand painted Sioux warriors appeared through the smoke of the burning grass, yelling and screaming, cranking off rounds from Henrys and Winchesters. They were firing from the hip as they ran. Swarthy figures, heavily muscled, they wore leather breeches and no shirts. Some wore large copper armlets around their bulging biceps.

Already there were soldiers and Sioux rolling in the grass, biting, pulling hair, grabbing at testicles. Teeth which some warriors had sharpened to points bit deeply into bearded necks, the warrior's head shaking at the grip like a terrier. The soldier would gouge the warrior's eyes with his thumbs, or try to fish hook his opponent's mouth and rip the face from the corner of the mouth.

Reno was grabbed from behind. A brown, tattooed arm, thickly corded with iron muscle constricted his windpipe as another horribly painted beast of a man hurled into him from the front with a murderous knife held low, preparatory to the disemboweling thrust.

"Let go! You're hurting me!" gasped the major, as he tried futilely to loosen the Samson-like arm, knotted with muscles that was crushing his larynx, "I can't fucking breathe!'

Reno grabbed his .45 and rammed it into the side of the man's head who was strangling him; he pulled the trigger and the resulting explosion ruptured his right ear drum.

"My ear! My God! I've ruptured my eardrum! I can't hear! I can't hear!" cried the officer.

Almost in the same motion he pulled back on the hammer spur again with his right thumb. He brought down the heavy revolver in an arcing motion and shot his knife wielding assailant in the side of the neck, just as the knife ripped through his belt leather. This left a horrible gash and threatened to unleash the hernia that resided uncomfortably close to the murderous laceration.

Two more pantherish figures armed with Winchesters leaped from the choking smoke and raced toward him.

"Help! Somebody!" shouted Reno as he reacted instinctively to the threats that were increasing as his command disintegrated.

The Indian with the neck wound staggered toward, and passed him, hand to neck, as the wound issued a high pressured spray of bloody mist between his taloned fingers.

The two advancing Indians raised their Winchesters, but Reno had the draw on the first one, a large Lakota Sioux, well over six feet in height. Reno fired from five feet and the brave reeled back, firing the Winchester high and to Reno's right. Then the major looked into the eyes of the man aiming the rifle straight at his forehead.

The thick, black hair was tightly woven into two pony tail braids and secured in place with rawhide. The forehead sloped back and was tattooed with images of a hieroglyphical design; over these was ocher based war paint. The eyebrows were shaved off and the eyelashes plucked out. The nose was aquiline but not long and the painted lips were pulled back revealing teeth sharpened to points. The warrior's mouth was open to regain breath as his lithe, well-defined abdomen rose and fell from the exertion of running.

All of this Reno was aware of during the fraction of the moment in which it all occurred.

"Don't do it!" commanded the Army officer.

The Lakota Sioux squeezed the trigger and Reno heard the hammer fall on an empty chamber as he continued the singular, fluid motion of pointing, and striking the hammer spur with the heel of his left hand while simultaneously squeezing the trigger with his right. The bullet rocketed from the 7 ½ inch barrel of the Colt and struck the brave in the sternum, smashing through it and knocking him back. He stepped back several times, holding one hand to his ruined sternum, and fell backward, holding onto the Winchester.

"To the wood line, men! All of you, now! Run for it!!!" screamed Reno.

Numerous troopers were horribly shot, and realized with cold horror that they were being left behind in the burning grass, to a fate worse than death…

« Chapter Twelve »

CUSTER WATCHED through DeRudio's binoculars from several miles away as the action unfolded at the south end of the Indian village. He turned the diopter focus rings until the imagery sharpened into stark clarity.

"Reno's doing a good job of it, and has the situation well in hand. Now, let's hop to it and hit 'em where they ain't!!! Martini, you get back there to Benteen and tell him there's a big village, and to link up with McDougal and bring the packs quick! Hold on a minute!"

Custer was agitated, stammering, and could not sit still in the saddle. Giovani Martini was not, to the Yellow Hair, a man who could think and rationalize, using common sense. He was more like one of his dogs that he could throw a bone to or teach simple tricks. But to expect the man to think was incomprehensible.

"Cooke, write it on a piece of paper for him, as the Wop cannot be trusted to convey the gravity of the situation!"

This order was to save Martini's life; Martini would be the only survivor of Custer's company. He had originally been assigned to Company H, but on the morning of the 25th had been reassigned temporarily to Custer's company as the bugler and orderly.

"I tell them the Indian flees before you, General!" shouted Martini.

Now he spurred his horse, aware of the importance of his mission, and worried that he might not find Benteen. He worried also that he might encounter Indians on the trail back, lots of them.

Once more, the General took in the clearness of the Montana air, the sight of cottonwoods and junipers that lined the Little Bighorn River, and the Douglas firs that festooned the distant mountainsides, the tops of which were, in 1876, ensconced with snow. The river, he could see, cut ravines one hundred feet deep in some places. The stone walls of the ravines were deeply fractured in places. Often small bushes grew from the cracks, cracks that contained more than a plant clinging tenaciously to the sheer rock wall; often rattle snakes sought refuge in those deeply fissured vaults. The treacherous ravines were orange in color and heavily outcropped with large boulders which balanced precariously where the angle relented enough to allow their presence. These stood out clearly through the Italian binoculars. Again he experienced a quick surge of desire to execute the flanking move, catching the red men unawares as they swarmed the furiously firing element of Major Reno.

Custer saw Reno's skirmisher's line being overwhelmed and studied the determined attackers with unease as Reno's thin line disintegrated and ran for the tree line. The ferocity of the Indian attack on Reno surprised the Boy General, and he reacted as he would have reacted in another time, in another place, namely Virginia.

The Yellow Hair had attacked Confederate positions using this same maneuver more times than he could remember, catching them unprepared throughout the dense forests and rolling hills of Virginia. He was positive the entire fighting force of the gargantuan encampment was attacking Reno and he would hit the village unchallenged.

"Come on! We have to move, there's no time to waste!" shouted General Custer.

Custer waved his hat at Major Reno and disappeared as he led his pitifully inadequate force in a tactically correct classical flanking movement. The former general who would have been President of the United States had the advantage of total surprise on his side, and absolutely nothing else.

Reno's soldiers coalesced in the tree line, prying out the swollen copper casings of their spent shells from the Springfield carbines. The extractors simply ripped through the soft, superheated copper casings.

Since the Civil War the Army saw breech loading weapons as the path into the 20th century. Firing a powerful buffalo dropping round and using fewer parts than a repeating rifle, it did well in controlled tests competing against other rifles. In 1872 the Army tested the Springfield against several domestic and foreign breech loading designs. A total of 99 rifles were inspected and tested, including Sharps, Peabody, Whitney, Spencer, Remington and Winchester.

The competition was held at the Springfield Armory, and to no one's surprise, Springfield won. Earlier versions of the Springfield rifles and carbines had utilized conversions of muzzleloaders with a trap door breech loading system designed by Erskine S. Allen, Master Armorer of the Springfield Armory. The trapdoor concept had been incorporated on 25,000 Springfield Model 1863s and refinements continued to be tweaked in, until the penultimate achievement was realized in the Allen trapdoor system; the Springfield Model 1873 was the fifth variation of the design.

The 7th Cavalry was issued the carbine version, sporting a 22 inch barrel and firing a black powder .45-55 caliber round. The massive 405 grain bullet was propelled at 1,100 feet per second, and its copper cartridge case, containing 55 grains of black powder, would swell and become stuck in the carbine's chamber. Since the carbine had no ramrod to remove the casing, soldiers always carried either a short bladed knife or other tool for shell extraction. It was the disaster that was unfolding at the Little Bighorn that later led to the Army's adoption of brass cartridges.

Certain wounded that had not been left behind were detailed to the task of removing stuck shells. Every able bodied man was firing from behind the concealment of buffalo berry brush, wild rose bushes and scrubby wild plum trees, others took cover behind the more substantial cottonwood trees, but these were landmarks for the Cheyenne and Sioux marksmen. The first thing Reno did when he got to the tree line was reload his Colt. Seeing that most of the horses were at the ready, he had to think quickly.

The Major knew that the big Colts were truly a godsend in that these belonged to the initial shipment in Colt's first contract with the Army. The fact that they happened to go to the 7th had to be Divine Providence, figured Reno, as he spun the weapon gunslinger style in his right hand, then stopped the motion in order to open the loading gate again and manually turn the cylinder, assuring himself that each cylinder bore had a .45 Long Colt in it.

The ejector housing was the first style with barrel boss and a round ejector rod head. The hammer was of the cavalry pattern and had elongated cross hatching on the face of the spur to aid in thumb cocking. The one piece black walnut stock had an oil finish. Each round nosed, soft lead bullet weighed 255 grains and was propelled by 40 grains of black powder. Unlike the continually jamming Springfield Carbine, the Colt .45's ejector rod reliably and efficiently removed the spent cartridge shells.

Blackened with soot, three to four thousand warriors low crawled forward on their bellies as well defined, deeply etched muscles rippled on their backs. Several thousand more maintained a suppressive fire. They were shooting Winchesters while mounted from horses. Others would kneel and then stand suddenly, firing, and then crouch back down.

"Officers up! Scouts up! Dammit get over here! Give me a sitrep!" Reno's voice was hoarse as he croaked the command.

Major Reno was at the base of a large box elder tree which was pock marked with bullet holes, the tail ends of many bullets plainly visible beneath the bark as more bullets splatted into it.

"Gimme a sitrrrrrrep!" growled Major Reno, looking from his cadre to his horses.

Lieutenants Varnum and Hodgson, along with several scouts, including Bloody Knife were in attendance. Suddenly, without warning, dozens of massively built Indians wearing war shirts with pockets bulging with ammunition penetrated the position from behind, armed with Henrys and Winchesters, shooting madly, point shooting without taking aim.

It was at this point that the thousands of blackened aboriginals leaped up and attacked at a full run into the anemic carbine fire of the Springfields. Reno's attention was drawn immediately to the threat at hand and without hesitation he began shooting his Colt Model 1873 revolver, scoring hits on six of the maddened brutes-they went down immediately, clutching their Winchesters and Henrys even as life ebbed from the piceous eyes. The scouts wrested the repeating rifles from the death grips of the monstrously strong hands.

Reno jerked Bloody Knife around, there was panic in his eyes, and spittle foamed at the corners of his mouth, reminding the superstitious Bloody Knife of a rabid man. Many such men he had seen, bitten by wild dogs, first with an aversion to water and later insanity would set in. Bloody Knife shook the thought from his mind as he fought down the fear that Reno inspired in him.

"Gimme a sitrep! What the hell! Where is Custer? He said he was bringing up the rear!" His voice betrayed the horror of the predicament as he began reloading the big service revolver. The entire wood copse had erupted into a maelstrom of thundering gunfire as the six shooting Colts played a symphony of havoc at point blank range on the infiltrating Sioux and Cheyenne.

Reno looked past Bloody Knife and saw a big Brule warrior aiming a Henry at him. Quickly, without thinking he sidestepped directly in front of Bloody Knife, placing Custer's favorite scout between himself and the enraged Brule. Bloody Knife's head exploded directly onto the face of Major Reno, who reacted reflexively, knocking down the bison like

Indian with a chest shot from his Colt. Sheer panic had set in and after grabbing Bloody Knife's Colt, he reloaded. Losing his nerve, Reno blasted four more braves off their feet with his Colt while running at a crouch to the horses.

"Men! Mount up! We're getting out of here!" Shouting excitedly, Reno swung onto his horse which leaped from the tree line before he had a chance to spur it.

The apparition of the cavalry major, whose face and hair was matted in blood and brain tissue, followed by any elements of his command that could mount a horse, surprised and unnerved the superstitious horde. The attacking mobs temporarily sought to dodge the horrific apparition followed by his minions. Other soldiers ran, holding to the saddles of the panicked horses as they tried to mount bunkie. This was a maneuver Custer had insisted his men practice; the rider would help the grounded cavalryman swing up and mount the horse. Sometimes it worked. Sometimes it didn't.

Many of the soldiers did not hear the order and they were horrified as word was passed they had been abandoned. Retreating in small groups, stopping to fire their Colts at the hundreds of pursuing braves and then run for their lives again. They made for the Little Bighorn River, sometimes hiding in blackberry thickets as ground sniffing Hunkpapa scented their trail, nose to ground, on all fours. Ruled by passion, the main body of thousands of horse mounted braves focused their attentions on the hundred or so of Reno's command. The faces of the warriors were masked in multicolored hues of war paints. War paints which could not hide the contorted, grimacing visages. Visages which conveyed the utmost antipathy toward the surviving elements of Reno's command who were fleeing to the highest hill on the opposite side of the river.

« Chapter Thirteen »

THE GROUND SHOOK with the vibrations of hundreds of war drums; the rumbling bombination was growing in crescendo. Through foggy banks of smoke appeared the silhouettes of women and children, some of whom fell to the revolver fire of the wounded soldiers who lay forgotten on the sweltering, smoke choked field. But when one silhouetted specter fell, a dozen more followed eerily from behind, to take its place. The thirty wounded soldiers left out in the open were roughly situated along the initial skirmishers line that Reno had established, and then abandoned when his position was being overwhelmed.

The teams were led by children armed with bow and arrows, and to the mix of thousands of children were hundreds of squaws, dressed in soft, loose fitting deerskins and armed with muzzle loading flintlocks or percussion cap rifles and muskets. The children would search for a soldier hiding in the grass, as a baby deer would hide, remaining perfectly still and hoping that silence will mislead its hunters. But with so many children milling about in the drifting smoke, there was no chance of being overlooked by the Indian youth, eager and excited as a white child on an Easter Egg Hunt.

Shrieks of glee and excitement would betray a wounded cavalryman, who more often than not responded with wildly pointed revolver fire at the figures darting and ducking in and out of the smoke from the grass fire. Dozens of children would launch arrows into the approximate area of grass from which the soldier's revolver fire issued. If some of the arrows found their mark, an Indian woman, most likely a Sioux, would be at the ready with a muzzle loader to shoot the wounded quarry if he bolted from cover. The Sioux women outnumbered the Cheyenne women by perhaps eight to one, as the mammoth Indian village was mainly a conglomeration of Sioux tribes; Brule, Hunkpapa, Minneconjou, Sans Arc, and Sihasapa.

The tribes had come together at the Little Bighorn on account of Sitting Bull's ability to prophecy. The tribes, they came in hundreds of clans connected along kinship lines. They came out of the mountains, the hills, grim faced stoic men who didn't smile. They came from the flat lands and prairies, thousands upon thousands. They came to hear the prophecies of a Holy Man who had risen from amongst the Lakota Sioux. A Holy Man whose name was spoken in awe, Sitting Bull.

Slashing and ripping at his arms in demonic fury, Sitting Bull called upon Wakan Tanka - the Great Spirit. As the Sun Dance drew on into an expanse of days, Wakan Tanka came to the Holy Man in a vision, and showed him the things to come.

"Low Dog!" Gall!! Crazy Horse!" Thundered the venerable Holy Man as he exploded from the human skinned tepee, "I have been spoken to! Bring to me your chieftains! Bring to me your fighting men and young boys who would be warriors! Bring them here!"

Although Sitting Bull had not eaten, drank or slept in seven days, he appeared as a man possessed. Hundreds, then thousands of warriors, followed by youths and women converged on the Lakota Holy Man.

"Wakan Tanka has spoken to me this day! The Great Spirit has given me sight!" roared Sitting Bull, his voice seemed to catch on the thin, hot breeze and be magnified. His high toned nasal inflections amplified and resonated as he emphasized the key point of his encounter. "I saw soldiers falling from the sky! Thousands of them, as though grasshoppers! We crushed them beneath our heel!"

Once a wounded soldier had been feathered with arrows, and brought down for good with a trade musket, he was disarmed and stripped of his boots and clothing. Then he would be dismembered-alive if possible.

Not everyone abandoned on the field were soldiers. Isaiah Dorman's life wasn't flashing before his eyes just yet. He had been overtaken on his wounded horse by a mix of Sioux and Cheyenne. He had twisted his torso and pointed his rifle while still on his mount; he unseated one of his antagonists with a rifle shot before his horse went down on top of him. His pursuers rode on past as others came up from behind.

Soldiers rode by him too, as he fired his Winchester carefully, aiming from the knee. Each shot brought down a painted, muscular figure. Dorman would stop firing and try to wave down a cavalryman so he could swing onto the horse and ride bunkie. Not concerned with saving the life of a Negro, the soldiers pushed his hands away when he'd grab for their saddle.

"Hey!" he shouted, "Gimme a hand here!" pleaded Dorman as he ran alongside a big sorrel mare mounted by a weasel faced, hatless soldier.

Dorman's lips were pulled back, exposing his white teeth. His mouth was open as he panted for breath, running alongside the big sorrel.

"Gimme a hand here! Lemme ride bunkie!" hollered the interpreter as he sprinted to keep up with the horse.

Custer had formally requested Dorman in writing as an interpreter back in May, because of his fluency in Sioux, Cheyenne and Arikawa (Cree). Dorman had not started out with the Custer column but had linked up with them at the Rosebud with a message. He had not been there long before he had spoken with Bloody Knife and thought of a reason to depart back to the fort, knowing the odds that were against the expedition.

"Hey! I said gimme a hand here!" shouted Dorman as he dropped back to the rear of the horse and grabbed it by the tail.

The soldier spurred the horse, causing it to lurch forward and free of Dorman's grasp. The sudden acceleration of the animal caused Dorman to fall forward face first into the scorched ground. Other fleeing soldiers road past him. He was drenched in sweat; his ears were ringing from gunfire. His nostrils flared as he breathed through his nose and mouth.

"Hold the fuck up! Don't go off and fucking leave me!"

When Custer caught on to Dorman's intentions, he had insisted he stay. Dorman had married into the Lakota tribe and was a personal friend of Sitting Bull, but none of this was on his mind when he took a round in the chest. The bullet smashed squarely into his sternum deflecting to the left, and bruising a lung. It was at this point that Isaiah thought for a moment of the Louisiana plantation he had been born into slavery on, and how fate had brought him here. Those thoughts were gone along with his rifle that was stripped from his hand and his revolver that was torn from his holster as braves robbed him of his possessions. Dorman struggled to regain the wind that had been knocked from him but could not.

He propped himself on one elbow and saw the Indian women coming, ten or eleven of them. The women circled him, striking him with stone hammers as he tried to shield himself. Rendered helpless with broken arms flailing obscenely about, the women stripped him and began slashing his thighs with skinning knives. His coffee cup was taken from his saddle bag, filled with his own blood, and hurled into his face.

« Chapter Fourteen »

FRED GERARD AND Billy Jackson hid in a blackberry bramble filled depression, having partially covered themselves with leaves and fallen branches. The hound like teams of Hunkpapa continued to sniff the ground, stopping to rise up on both knees and scent the smoke filled air, which mingled with the rank, decaying litter of the ground. The sweet smell of the burning grass combined with the harsher odors of burning trees as the fire encroached into the thick tree line and established itself.

Confused by the compounding of scents, the man hounds continued on, uncertainly. Behind them followed a column of lithe, muscular warriors, looking from side to side, each carried a Winchester or Henry in one hand, their other hand moving the branches of trees and undergrowth aside as they prowled the riverside hunting for fugitives.

Suddenly, one of the men stopped, and looked directly at the bramble in which Gerard and Jackson lay hidden. He was a morbidly painted, tattooed, and heavily muscled man of average height. He was shirtless, and wore a bandolier of bullets for the Winchester he gripped in his right hand. Around his bull neck depended a necklace of bear teeth. Gerard could make out the swell of the warrior's biceps under the armlets of beaten copper. A cavalryman's belt sustained a pair of buckskin breeches on the lean loins of the warrior. Into the belt was thrust a large hunting knife. Although clearly Brule, he had Caucasian facial features. The head was shaven but for a large scalp lock in the center. He continued to stare for a moment, and then moved on. Gerard cursed himself for averting his vision too late; it was widely held that a person could sense being stared at.

Fredrick Frances Gerard was Custer's civilian interpreter for the Arikawa (Cree) scouts. Having married the sister of Whistling Bear, he spoke the language fluently, and was capable in dialects of Sioux, Cheyenne, and to a lesser extent, Arapaho. He surveyed with uneasy scrutiny the menacing gloom of the darkening haunts, in which the trees sometimes assumed the figures of men. A hazy gray mist of fog mixed with smoke made vague the misshapen, malformed silhouettes of the trees. The riperine forest was transforming itself into a menagerie of unimaginable horrors with the setting of the sun.

"How do we get out of here?" asked Jackson.

Jackson was a Blackfoot scout and the grandson of a white fur trader. His hair was cut short in the way of the white soldiers and his long, narrow face reflected his European ancestry; dark complexioned, tall and thin, he was often mistaken for a ranchero. He had lost his hat, and was wearing a black shirt with matching trousers; the cuffs were not tucked into his black leather Wellington boots.

"Not wise to follow those painted devils," murmured Gerard, biting the corner from a plug of thickly pressed tobacco.

"We'll try picking up a trail once the moon comes up. When the wind shifts, it will blow the smoke from the grass fires to a different direction. This will give us enough moonlight to approach the river. Beaver trails will let us know when we're near to it." Gerard continued.

Upon exiting the copse of trees, Reno rode at breakneck speed nearly two miles alongside the river, followed by his entourage and the hotly pursuing Lakota, Cheyenne and Arapaho. He had seen a high bluff on the other side of the Little Big Horn, it was periodically visible through the haze of the growing blaze of the grass fire, which was now towering in red waves of fifty and a hundred feet. As the wind whipped it up, it fed ruthlessly off the tall grasses, weeds and shrubs.

The heavy war horses of the 7th reached the river's edge and without halting leaped fifteen feet into the chilled water, submerging with their riders and coming back up. Hundreds of Indians raced alongside the cavalry, taking unsteady shots with Henrys and Winchesters, but the single action Colts demanded a respect that kept the painted braves from realizing full capability of their repeating rifles. Other horribly painted hordes had crossed the river and were on the higher ground, shooting into Reno's men as they tried to mount the steep slope.

Overcome with the killing lust, a seething mass of red men descended the bluffs, hurling themselves into the troopers, many of whom were dismounted and climbing ashore, as water sloshed from the tops of the filled boots. Three massively built braves went for the mounted Reno; one of them grabbed the reins of his horse, while another slashed at his leg with a bowie knife, cutting deeply into the leather of the high legged cavalry boot, drawing blood. The third was a gigantic beast of a man with two eagle feathers fixed into the rawhide braid of his gray streaked black hair. He fired his Henry at the wildly careening Reno, leaving a furrow along the length of Reno's scalp giving the appearance of the hair having been parted as though with a comb. Quickly fine threads of blood sprang from the white tissue, which welled up with blood.

"To me, men! I am beset!" Reno shouted.

As he screamed the terrified words he drew and fired his .45 into the rock hard slab of chest muscle shielding the heart of the Henry wielding warrior.

The bullet struck the gorilla-like Brule as the behemoth ejected and cranked another .44 caliber round into the deadly repeater. Panicking, Reno brought the big revolver from his right, to the left and over the saddle horn pointing the 7 and ½ inch barrel a foot from the slashing warrior's face, which was painted black on the bottom half, and red on the upper. Thumb cocking the hammer spur and pulling the trigger, he saw the back of the warrior's head erupt in an explosion of blood and bone fragments, the brain oozed out and dropped into the buffalo grass. Not realizing it was dead, the body just stood there, hand gripping the knife hilt, uplifted.

"Save me!" screamed Reno, as he took unsteady aim at the big Lakota who still held onto the rein of the rearing horse, the thickly corded muscles of his arms standing out with the effort.

Time seemed to move slowly in the mind of the bison like warrior as he studied the face of the man who was about to kill him. Reno's face was a mask of blood and brain tissue from Bloody Knife, added to that was the obscene part in his hair, all of it contributed to a horrific grotesque image that froze the warrior in place, he could not avert his gaze nor release the reins.

"I am beset!" shouted Reno at the top of his lungs.

The major squeezed the trigger and the slug struck the man near the very top of his head, shearing it off. The warrior released the reins and instinctively reached for the top region of his skull, picked out a piece of brain matter, studied it for a fraction of a second and ran away screaming. Hundreds of the other painted men witnessed this, and their killing ardor gave way to a superstitious fear, which developed into panic. They looked at the horrific visage of Reno, who returned the stare-the stare of a madman, screaming:

"Men! To me! Be of assist!"

At first, dozens of warriors, then hundreds began to flee the field, to escape this hellish apparition that could not be unseated from his horse.

« Chapter Fifteen »

BEYOND THE LITTLE Bighorn River the primitive still held suzerainty over the gloomy haunts of the tree lines, and in buffalo skinned tepees where the scalps of soldiers hung. The coals of cooking fires glowed redly, casting gruesome shadows on leather walls. Drums thundered, and Winchesters were cleaned in the hands of red, solemn men with braided black hair and obsidian eyes. Many of those eyes glared malevolently toward the hill atop which Major Reno had reestablished his command, while others, wearing green war paint which they believed assisted with night vision, scoured the woods that lined the Little Big Horn.

Gerard and Jackson had resumed their journey toward the Little Bighorn River in an oblique direction; not heading directly for it, but carefully feeling their way through the forest at an angle, to avoid the numerous search parties. Both of the escapees froze in their tracks as a long, sustained hissing sound passed directly over their heads. The sound was made by the air rushing through the plumage of a great horned owl, dimly illuminated by the growing moonlight. The heavily built, barrel shaped bird alit on a somber tree branch of a gnarled cottonwood and issued a "hooo ha hooo, hoo haaaa whoooooo!" this was quickly answered by others, further away, and still more, throughout the canyons that enclosed the Little Bighorn. Soon the calls of owls became deafening as their numbers grew exponentially.

"It's Sitting Bull!" cursed Gerard. Jackson felt the hairs on the back of his arms stand up in the horror of the import of what Gerard expostulated.

"You mean? You can't be serious!"

"Keep your voice down" muttered Gerard, "yes, he's using the owls to track us, and now he knows where we're at. We must make at once for the river with all that we're worth. He is onto us now, and more will be following. Let's go, we've got to run for our lives!"

The indigo serpent that was the Little Bighorn glided and snaked its way through the wood lined canyons and ravines, flanked by ghostly gulches in the silver wash of moonlight. With its binocular vision, the owl telescoped its keen eyesight onto the two figures making their way through the trees, behind them, it saw, was a pack of two dozen large wolves, hotly pursuing the trail.

The pack was led by an enormous alpha male. The wolves howled insanely at the warming scent of the two vagabonds, growling and snapping their jaws at each other when one would impede the progress of the other. The fugitives espied dead trees, whose trunks had been girdled by beaver, and they used these as guide marks in their headlong race to the river, abandoning all pretenses at silence. The ground suddenly inclined sharply and the two slid into the chilled night waters of the Little Bighorn, the reflections of the stars and moon shattered violently before returning to their unstable positions atop the sluggishly moving waters. The arriving wolves slid into the water as the scree of clayey limestone and friable sandstone made untenable the purchase of pawed feet.

Other wolves, which did not slide on the loose rock into the river, leapt into it, swimming furiously at Jackson and Gerard. "Swim for it!" shouted Gerard "We've gotta make for the other side before they get us!"

"Wolves can't do this!" cried Jackson, who recalled seeing with horror human like eyes staring at him above the maw of one of the wolves as it swam doggedly toward him. Treading water with every ounce of strength, they caught the current and were swept into a vortex of eddies and whirlpools in one of the river's rapids. Seven or eight miles downstream they managed to stumble ashore, scrambling up the moonlit scree-a jumble of lignite and shattered sheets of slate. Many fine specimens of petrified wood glowed eerily in the wash of the moon, ghosts of an ancient, primordial forest. They froze in place behind the fallen trunk of a gigantic petrified tree. There followed a tense silence in which Jackson could hear his pulse pounding in his ears.

There were guttural expostulations just beyond the next column of shattered petrified timber, then sparks of flint and a flash of gunpowder ignited the dried tinder-illuminating a group of four painted aboriginals clustered around a nascent cooking fire. This sprung brightly into life as the flames took hold. All four were wearing war shirts and breeches made of deerskin, the shirts were adorned with curious designs. Gerard and Jackson spied in silence, watching the group prepare a macabre meal; a captured trooper lay dead nearby.

The dead soldier was occasionally visible in the unsteady light cast by the fire's wildly dancing flames. Using a hatchet-the kind acquired at trading posts, one of the braves hacked through the sternum, and flayed the rib cage open. Using a small hunting knife, he carefully removed the lungs of the soldier. These were wrapped in green corn husk sheaths and placed at the fire's edge. As the four continued their subdued conversation, the meat cutter stood up and walked toward the river to clean his hatchet, knife, and hands.

Short and stocky, the man's war shirt failed to ensconce the hard, muscular lines of his arms and chest. He walked with the bow legged gait of one who had spent his life mounted on horseback. His black hair was pulled back tightly and braided into a pony tail that was secured with rawhide. A single large eagle feather jutted at an angle above where the braid began. The forehead slanted sharply back and was flattened across the front. Across the deformed forehead writhed a single red horizontal zigzag made of iron oxide. The eyebrows were shaved off, the pupils were of coal, and the sclera bloodshot and reddened. The nose was long and evilly hooked. Nearly the entirety of the lower face was masked with a black human hand imprint, derived of charcoal mixed with saliva and buffalo fat. His thin lips pulled back as he spat tobacco juice, revealing an absence of frontal dentation, except for the horribly emphasized canine teeth. He swung past the petrified log where the two fugitives lay, holding their breaths, not looking directly at, but peripherally past the danger which did not discern their presence.

The Oglala Sioux knelt at the water's edge, cleaning his instruments, when a subtle sound alerted his ears. He jumped upright and turned his head sharply in the same motion, the tendons standing out in the thickly corded muscles of his ox-like neck. He froze in place, staring into the aqua blue eyes of the grey timber wolf; it was a huge, yet slender and powerfully built animal. Its rib cage was large and deeply descending. The abdomen was pulled in and the shoulders and neck were powerfully muscled.

Other wolves appeared from the river's edge, violently shaking the water from their coats, while more appeared from out of the tree line, smiling with tongues lolling out of their mouths as they panted. Seeing that the flat headed Indian was not his quarry, the large alpha male began to turn, eliciting a high pitched yell from the brave alerting his companions. The three Oglalas at the cooking fire began firing almost immediately at the wolves, cranking out rounds from the Winchesters and Henrys with such rapidity that the pack was devastated, the leader being hit mortally behind the shoulder.

Instantly, in a large tepee centered in one of the giant concentric circles of the Indian village, Sitting Bull lurched from his self-induced coma, howling like a wolf. The remaining pack members-fully a dozen of them, rushed the three warriors at the fire side. Their ammunition expended and not having time to reload, they could not ignore the heavy, broad foreheads from which protruded long and powerful jaws. These were armed with oversized teeth and were capable of exerting a crushing pressure of nearly two tons per square inch. Instinctively hugging close to the fire, the three red men savagely swung their rifles as clubs and yelled at the wolves. The flat headed man fled in silence, his receding presence betrayed by the movement of gravel beneath moccasined feet. Gerard and Jackson ran for the river, the reflection of the moon and stars being shattered once again...

Re-emerging on the opposite side, and beyond the next serpentine bend in the river, Jackson and Gerard mounted the steeply sloped bank by clutching onto the branches of trees which leaned precariously toward the water; the river having undercut and carried away their supporting soil. Often root masses were exposed which clung tenaciously in the fissures of stone, sometimes the caverns of beavers would extend into the mud and clay that punctuated imbedded boulders and rock.

The two scout-interpreters avoided skin ripping thorns and low hanging branches with effort.

They were pushing through thick undergrowth and making more noise than they wanted. It was slow, terrifying work. From behind them came the screams of the three warriors, who were being devoured alive by the wolves. The screams carried in the night, echoing in the canyons until they were swallowed by the concussion of the thundering Indian war drums. The silvery light of the full moon reflected eerily off the snowcapped mountain tops in the distance, as hundreds of wolf packs consisting of dozens of individuals each howled to each other. Their eyes glowed when they looked to the moon as they serenaded.

The howls of one group were answered by those of another, all along the Little Bighorn River, until the whole length of waterway was a cacophony of howling. The orchestra was magnified and reverberated by horrifying echoes throughout the canyons. Dark hands continued to pummel painted war drums as a chorus of frogs and crickets chimed into the opus.

The aroma of roasting sacrificial human flesh added an odd smell to the cacophony of sound, as it wafted down from the village. Dead soldiers were being spitted and roasted over large beds of coals, their fat dripped onto the embers resulting in violent hissing clouds of smoke, which the wind caught and carried to the flared nostrils of Gerard and Jackson.

They had penetrated some distance into the purple gloom of the woods when Jackson asked Gerard, "Is Sitting Bull in league with the Devil?"

Gerard shook his head in the negative. "I've heard it rumored that Sitting Bull is well known within Occult circles back East, in Boston. Here, take a bite out of this plug. Careful of those loose teeth, though."

Jackson accepted the plug of tobacco from Gerard, and biting into the thickly pressed licoriced brick, bit off a piece. "Then, he has eyes everywhere and we have no chance of escape." postulated Jackson, as he pushed one of his upper incisors back into alignment. He hoped that the tobacco would kill the gnawing hunger pains that the smell of roasting meat had evoked.

Gerard was silent for a moment, and when he replied it was with carefully chosen words.

"He can't be everywhere at once. Reno's bunch made it to the river, and the last I saw of them, were attempting to make for the high hill on the opposite side. There may still be soldiers in the woods, yet. And as to Custer-well assuming he is still alive, that will be yet another random factor in the equation for Sitting Bull.

I heard heavy firing from the direction I saw Custer go. Into that maelstrom of musketry is where most of the braves went. One man's loss is another man's gain, and to Custer we undoubtedly owe our lives."

Jackson intentionally swallowed the saliva mixed with tobacco juice, willing his hunger to stop.

"I speculate, then, as to what Sitting Bull is doing at this very moment?" worried Jackson.

« Chapter Sixteen »

MARGARET SAT ON ONE of the chairs of the bedroom, dressed in matching beige walking shirt and skirt, underneath was a hoop underskirt. These were held in place by a narrow, black velvet belt. She was not wearing a corset and she had taken her shoes off at the door. Her legs were crossed and fingers laced behind her neck as she watched Libbie undress. Even though she was 23 now, she still liked to watch her older sister in law in the act of undressing, a practice she had indulged in since her teens, when timidly, she first asked permission to observe.

It was midmorning now, and the sun was beaming brightly through the tall window panes of the bay room and light spilled into the parlor. The glass panes were a foot wide and two feet tall, there were four of these windows one atop the other, each divided by a window frame. There were six rows of these tall windows side by side, which if viewed from the outside conveyed the impression of an octagon which seemed to extrude itself partially from the side of the house.

Potted orchids and ferns sat atop a two tiered table which resembled an end piece of a sofa. Usually this table and other potted verdure were positioned on the floor of the bay room to capture the maximum exposure to sunlight. During social functions these would be relocated strategically for maximum visual appeal. These had been moved aside and a small pallet was situated on the mahogany floor in such a way that it was totally illuminated by the glass filtered sun. Each tier of windows had its own spring loaded window shade, which was completely rolled up, affording the maximum entry of sunlight. The bay room extended outward from between the two massive fireplaces located in the east wall of the parlor. Margaret always looked forward with great anticipation to the mornings when Libbie would sprawl naked atop the pallet in the full sun of the bay room windows.

"Libbie, I don't know where you gather the courage for such brazen frankness, never could I produce the boldness to lay before the sun as do you. And here I am your most devoted audience! I cannot but anticipate with all the excitement in the world, your sunbathing sessions!" expostulated Margaret, who noted how the sun was amplified through the window glass, causing sweat to bead up and pool into the small of Libbie's back.

"It's alright to be shy, Margaret. It's alright to watch me." responded Libbie, relishing the heat of the amplified sun rays that beamed through the glass windows.

Above the wooden mantel of the fireplace was mounted the trophy head of a buffalo, whose skin had been fashioned into a coat which served at times as a comforter on the master bedroom bed. Black eyes made of glass peered from either side of the head of the wooly beast. Its appearance was made gruff by the presence of a large goatee underneath the jaw.

As Margaret Custer padded by on bare feet to get Libbie a glass of water, the lifeless eyes did not seem in fact to be so lifeless; they seemed able to see. As a matter of fact, there were many trophies mounted on the walls of the house, some in every room. There was the grizzly bear, whose head graced the wall above Custer's study; in 1872 the General had acquired the trophy while at the Yellowstone River, in the company of Alexis-the fourth son of the Tsar of Russia. This bear's skin often served as a rug before one or the other of the two fireplaces in the parlor.

These trophies and souvenirs were often rearranged, being moved from one wall to another or from one room to the next. There were the mounted heads of deer, of antelope, stuffed trophies of feathered varieties stood perched on wall mounts, or atop tables that were lined with porcelain figurines or framed photos. One of Custer's favorite was a beautiful snowy owl-a female belonging to one of the largest species in North America. He spent hours in the winter months practicing his hobby of taxidermy.

Returning from the kitchen with a large glass of water, Margie's loosely contained breasts jiggled as she passed the Steinway square rosewood grand piano, beside which stood a magnificent harp-both rented from Minnesota and delivered via Conestoga wagon. The reflections of daily life in the Custer household played in the glass eyes of the stuffed animals; eyes that seemed uncannily alive. Eyes through which a Hunkpapa Lakota holy man watched, from a large tepee far away, surrounded by lithe brown naked maidens.

On December 22, 1870, the powerful medicine man and noted prophet, Sitting Bull had accurately predicted a total eclipse of the sun. Whether or not he'd been privied on the event by occult circles of the whites was never ascertained. But what is certain, is that the tribes of the Sioux and Cheyenne, as well as many others believed he accurately predicted it, and that it was a portent of the total destruction of the European tidal wave of immigration. The destruction of the very people Sitting Bull gazed upon now, through the eyes of mounted trophies.

Neither Libbie nor Margie Custer was aware of this as they discussed the upcoming event of the morrow. Libbie stood up, the pool of sweat running down the small of her back and into the large crack of her plump behind as she accepted the proffered glass of warm water. Draining the glass, she lay down on her back to give sun to her front.

"Tomorrow we will be clad in rustling silk gowns, light gloves and shall carry our parasols. We will bring our picnic and Et-nah-wah-ruchta along with her husband and sundry family members will accompany us. There is to be creek fighting and our little group of excited women, lifted up by one common impetus, will seek delight in gathering by the stream to revel in the excitement!" chirped Elizabeth, excitedly.

Margaret listened with genuine surprise as Libbie described the contest. She was sitting on the two person double end, upholstered sofa fanning herself. She felt the room was uncomfortably hot, and unbuttoned the top two buttons of her walking shirt, her heavy breasts were glistening with sweat, and she had to admire Libbie's endurance under the intense magnified heat pouring through the glass panes.

"But what is creek fighting? Is this a game or some recreation indulged in by our aboriginal friends?" asked Margaret, who felt nauseous but resisted the urge to pass out.

"Libbie, I am feeling faint, how much longer can you endure this session with father sol?" asked Margaret as she lay down on the small sofa, fanning herself harder; she turned her head toward Libbie and watched a pool of sweat form on the flat of Libbie's stomach beneath the small breasts, which she thought seemed almost boyish when she lay on her back like that.

"Libbie, I believe I am near to passing out!" gasped Margaret as she felt the room spinning, prompting her to lay down flat on her back.

Margaret awoke thirty minutes later, feeling the wetness of a dampened bath cloth across her forehead and other wet cloths across her chest and feet. Libbie had opened the bay room windows and a warm, but cooling breeze entered the parlor. Grasshoppers lined the rusted window screens. All of the other windows had been opened. The two front doors had been opened as well; the outer screened doors acting as barriers to the swarms of grasshoppers, permitting a cross breeze.

"I am so sorry, sister." Libbie apologized. She was dressed now, wearing a light blue summer dress. It had an arrangement of wide tucks on the bodice and skirt. She fanned Margaret with a plume of peacock feathers.

"I am so set to my sessions in the bay-room that incognizance impeded my awareness of the torrid heat in this house. Try to sit up slowly and take sips from this glass of water." The high ceilings assisted with the dispersion of the heat.

"How are you feeling, now?" asked Libbie who was now seated on the piano stool as she continued to fan Margaret.

"I feel deeply embarrassed, and melancholied by the imposition my swoon has burdened you with."

replied Margaret, who felt better with the fresh air circulating in the large, high ceilinged room.

Margaret indeed felt much better, although weak. Libbie continued talking to Margaret in her cooing manner as she fanned her.

"I implore you to remain for the extent of the day. Et-nah-wah-ruchta will be by to cook and prepare my bath. She is as near to being a sister as an Indian girl possibly can be. Together we will reconstitute your vitality for the event of tomorrow." Libbie assured Margaret who saw the full, pretty lips form an O as she blew air on her face. The chin was small, the jawline well set. The smallish nose was met on either side by rounded cheeks, above which resided soft, gray blue eyes. Her eyebrows were plucked into thin wisps beneath a high forehead. Auburn hair, damp and smelling of sweat, fell to her shoulders.

The smell of Elizabeth's sweat reminded Margaret of the odor of pork sausage frying in a skillet; the odor seemed to hang in the air around her, creating a mental image of kitchen smells of bacon and sausage. Margaret's nausea and faintness were being replaced with hunger and desire.

"Tell me of the coming event tomorrow, Libbie. For if the heat will be equal to that of today, I fear to be an embarrassment." requested Margie as Libbie continued to fan her.

"I promise that tomorrow you will find surcease to your melancholy. Of the event in the creek tomorrow I am inexpressibly impatient. There is a beautiful young Indian maiden of the Arikawa, who has the propitious misfortune to be serenated by two handsome young warriors-both of whom are dashing young scouts for my dear husband, the General. Oh! How they would be with him now, had they not been sent on an errand of utmost urgency to secure provisions for the gallant families who sadly remain sequestered at this garrison! Rather than choosing the one, and thereby alienating the other, she has elected to have them both sport in the creek for her."

"Do you imply that the Indian girl means that they fight for her?" asked Margie, her curiosity piqued.

"Why yes, Margie." Libbie smiled angelically, "It is an athletic contest in which the victor will sound the death knell over his competitor, restraining him beneath the agitated waters until he is compelled to relinquish his breath!"

Margaret did not reply immediately. Finishing the glass of water, she sat the empty glass atop the end table, watched by the eyes of the antelopes mounted on the wall opposite her.

"But I have seen the Indians swim and flaunt their nakedness quiet brazenly, Elizabeth. In modesty I have turned my face and hurried away. In the endeavor of the two suitors to subdue one another I dread bearing witness to the exposure of their parts, which scarcely can be hid in their Neptunic struggle. To see such appendages flopping madly about would be a visage of the utmost humiliation to a proper lady, such as yourself."

The rising and falling motion of the peacock feathers reflected on the black, marble eyes of the twin trophies of prong horned antelope. A thousand miles away, in a large tepee lay a sweating, comatose man, also being fanned. Brown nubile virgins, whose naked bodies glistened with sweat, fanned the medicine man with shields made of buffalo hide. Naked but for a loin cloth, the sorcerer's breathing was erratic, coming in short, shallow breaths, it would stop-for up to a minute, then resume. Sometimes the breathing was characterized by a long drawn out breath, which would be followed by several rapid inspirations, then slow almost to a stop again. The charcoal eyes stared intensely into the blue void beyond the circle of the hole in the top of the tepee. Far above was a buzzard, through whose eyes was focused the intense concentration of the sorcerer below, eyes which transported the imagery of what reflected from the eyes of the mounted antelope.

The eyelids closed, and the black dot that was the buzzard drifted away, carried aloft by thermal waves that issued from a half mile below. From the buzzard's view was an oblong semicircle dragging for more than four miles along the serpentine Little Bighorn River. Within the semicircle were more than a half dozen massive circles. Such was the extent of the enormous village; a conglomeration of many tribes-such as the world had never seen, nor would ever see again.

Lakota, Northern Cheyenne, and Arapaho had come together in response to the magic of the man who was lying inside the tepee prostrate on bare ground;

the buffalo skins on the floor of the tepee were moved to either side of him. Slowly emerging from his catatonic state, Sitting Bull's eyelids opened, after mumbling words in his native tongue.

"The Yellow Haired One is not there!" shouted the enraged seer who then lay exhausted.

He was a massively built man, even while supine, one could see that he stood a head and shoulder taller than most braves. His unbraided hair was parted down the middle, and lay about his broad shoulders on a carpet of turned earth. The soil of which seemed incongruous with the alkaline soil of this area. The soil of the tepee floor appeared as though it came from elsewhere.

His chest rose and fell rhythmically as his normal respirations returned, the swell of massive pectoral muscles underscored the vitality of the life force ebbing back into his lungs. The neck, as thick as a buffalo's, supported a head which bore a horrific visage; the forehead was high, and the dark skin was furrowed with deep lines. The eyebrows and lashes had been plucked smooth and into the bleary sclera of the eyes were set dilated pupils. Everything curved downward on the face, lending to the impression of a gigantic frown; the pronounced crow's feet at the corner of the eyes curved downward, the enormous cartilaginous nose hooked viciously downward, as did the corners of the thin, cruel lips. The jawline was strong, and the chin pronounced. The darkly pigmented face was horrifically pitted with countless, deep, scars of small pox. These covered the entire face, including the nose. Rolling over onto his stomach, he assumed the front leaning rest position, and pushed himself up with heavily muscled arms-the triceps standing out like horseshoes with the exertion, like Antaeus he seemed to gain his strength from the earth.

"Send to me, Low Dog! Do it now! Move!" shouted the magician, reinvigorated with the power flooding back into him.

« Chapter Seventeen »

CAPTAIN BENTEEN FOLDED the note and placed it into his left shirt pocket, resuming march at the head of his mounted column of five officers and 110 men. They were moving rapidly toward the sound of heavy gunfire. It was the sound of many different weapons types. The smell of burning grass mixed with gunpowder increased as the column drew near.

Approaching the Little Bighorn River, Benteen saw chaos in the field as Reno's command desperately blasted their way through and established themselves on the hill. The captain had sent a man back to Captain McDougal's column to urge them forward with the ammunition packs. Benteen then swung back around to the reverse slope of the hill that Reno's men were occupying.

"Have the men standby to receive orders to formation immediately! Every fourth man takes bridles. I'll tell you what to do in a moment!" Captain Benteen gently spurred his horse up the slope of the massive hill, the acrid smoke making his eyes water.

Major Reno rushed down the slope to meet Benteen, grabbing him by the leg. Benteen struck the hand of his superior officer with a sharp smack of his riding crop, causing Reno to grab the smarting hand with his other.

"You've got to help us! Half of my men are dead! We're out of ammunition!" pleaded Major Reno; his voice was shrill, and hard to hear over the sound of gunfire.

"Put your hand on me again and I'll rip it off! I've got a note from Custer to join him ASAP with the pack mules and I've sent a man back to stick a hot poker up McDougal's ass! What the hell's happened here?" ejaculated the junior officer as he surveyed the situation before him.

"Get your companies into position facing the river!" screamed Benteen, anger was in his voice, anger and exasperation.

"But..."Reno vacillated.

Leaning forward, the Captain struck the major smartly across the ear of which the drum had been perforated, causing Reno to drop to his knees, both hands placed on the ear, screaming in pain.

"If you don't get your men into position now, I'll kill ya!" shouted the exacerbated Benteen.

There were thousands of red men swarming the area-they were everywhere. Benteen was torn between orders from Custer and a situation that had been radically altered since those orders were written.

Soon they'll be over the hill and finish us off. Reno's out of ammo. I've got to deploy my men with his around this hill, before they overrun us! the captain was thinking to himself.

Benteen considered the situation before him; Reno's ragged command was desperately arranging a defensive perimeter about the hill, there was considerable gunfire directed onto the soldiers from thousands of Indians some distance away, and a couple of miles distant he could hear a murderous fire fight in progress. He had orders from Custer that Reno just now countermanded.

Not that Benteen had any compunction about bucking Reno's orders; it just seemed that now might be a fortuitous moment to obey them. Captain Benteen shouted loudly, ensuring that the dialogue would be heard.

"Be clear, Major Reno! Are you countermanding Lt Colonel Custer's order? Are you ordering me to remain here with you to save your command from annihilation? Is that an order?"

"Yes!" shouted Reno, "are you blind to this disaster unfolding?"

Quickly, without hesitation Captain Benteen trotted back down to the base of the hill and issued orders to his adjutant and 1st Sergeant.

"Deploy the companies around this side of the hill, tying in with Reno's men, make it quick, and give orders to divide your ammo with them. McDougal will be here in half an hour with the pack train!"

Captain McDougal with two officers, 127 soldiers and seven civilian packers arrived as Benteen's Companies D, H, and K tied in with what remained of Reno's Companies A, G, and M. McDougal's men tied in as well. Soon after, a detachment under Lt. Weir departed to join with the Custer group, other elements were detached from the redoubt also, and mounted up with the intent to rush to Custer. Several coordinated rifle volleys had been heard coming from the Custer element. The rifle volley was an accepted and understood means of signaling for assistance.

Atop the next hill, Weir, Benteen and Reno surveyed the cloud of dust and the positions of what appeared to be at least one Custer redoubt being overwhelmed. Lowering their binoculars a few degrees, they saw undulations in the grass, as though the ocean of green was being whipped about by a strong wind. Squinting his eyes while trying to focus the image of the rudimentary binoculars, Reno realized with cold, clammy horror what it was.

Reno drew and fired his revolver high, without taking aim, startling the other two officers who scowled at him, and then returning their view to the anomaly a thousand yards ahead of them; they saw a figure drop from a spotted Indian pony-a one in a million lucky shot. It was then that they realized the sheer enormity of what was approaching them, as they turned their mounts, they saw that Reno had already descended to the rear at a fast trot and was screaming orders at the top of his lungs to take cover in the positions that the troopers had been hastily preparing.

On every side of the hill waves of Indians climbed the bluffs. Some low crawled, seeking to evade the accurate rifle fire, while others ran uphill at a low crouch, their Winchesters and Henrys held in one hand, so that they could break their fall with the other if they had to go to ground. Some, armed only with trade muskets had discharged their one shot and came on armed only with knives. They came to hand grips with the soldiers, shouting maniacally. All along the crest of the hill the fighting raged out of control, manifested by its primitive ferocity.

It seemed through Reno's sweat stung eyes that he looked down into an ocean of red calamity when suddenly from behind him a mob of howling Sioux and Cheyenne broke through the perimeter and flooded into the center of the knoll. Hundreds of horses and dozens of wounded were packed in there. War bonnets flying, many wore decorated deer skin leather war shirts, or were bare-chested but for a reed vest. Others were naked except for a loin cloth, the quivering, over-developed muscles of their arms standing out in bold relief as they strangled wounded soldiers.

132

"My Lord!" screamed Reno, "They have broken through!"

Half a dozen heavily muscled Hunkpapa Sioux rushed toward Reno, two of them firing Henrys from hip level as they ran, striking the paltry force rushing to assist the major. Reacting blindly, Reno fired indiscriminately, a slug shattered the flint stone of a coup stick, its deadly shrapnel imbedding into dark, atramentous eyes and the thick, vein distended torsos of bull necks.

"Ha! To me men! I am beset!" implored Reno-the seven and one half inch barrel lifted with each detonation of the searingly hot Colt. A massively built Brule, standing a full head above six feet, approached Reno, flinging down a dripping scalp lock and slipping .44 caliber cartridges into the loading gate of his Winchester Yellowboy as he walked. He was laughing. The hammer of Reno's Single Action Army fell upon a spent chamber, and he looked into the blood shot sclera and black pupils of a man whose eyes beamed into him.

"To me, men!" reiterated the major, while all around him men rolled about locked in deadly embrace, the outcome of the hill was in the balance, Major Reno could not receive succor and had to think fast.

Reno took the last dreg of whiskey from his flask and hurled it at the approaching Brule Sioux, who deftly canted his head to one side, allowing the object to pass.

"Get away from me!" warned the major, his rat like eyes were slits behind squinted eye lids, eyelids which dare not close for even a second as the macabre threat approached.

"I like killin' funny man!" shouted the Brule Sioux over the din of gunfire, raising the Winchester to his shoulder, "Gonna take your hair!"

The man wore a large war bonnet of eagle feathers, horse hair and buffalo hair. It was split with buffalo horns and rested on the head by means of a deer skullcap cushioned with rabbit skin. The brow band consisted of trade beads and hawk bells. Reno did not notice any hair, nor the forehead which was ensconced by the magnificent headdress. He was aware that the Brule had no eye brows and that the nose was a pronounced arch, hooking evilly downward. The face was masked in red war-paint, and had a white lightning bolt extending from either eye, downward to the corners of the cruel mouth; the lips of which were pulled back, revealing a set of straight, tobacco stained teeth as he aimed the Winchester. The defined jaw was set upon a neck which had the girth of a tree trunk. Crisscrossing the swell of the massively developed pectoral muscles were two bandoliers of rifle ammunition. The muscles of the abdomen were sharply defined and tightly pulled in. Both biceps were barely contained by large armlets of beaten copper.

"Now, fat white man, you die!" yelled the Brule, the stock weld was slippery as he pressed the side of his cheek into the sweaty rifle stock, jerking the trigger impatiently.

The first bullet passed through the jowl of Reno's neck, on the right side. Turning his head from the flash of the weapon, the second round penetrated the cheek of the left side of his mouth, between the upper and lower pallets, demolishing his dentures. Reflexively, Reno swung his head back and spat out the dentures, and locked eyes with the brave, who looked at the dentures, and then at Reno.

"See what you did?" the words came across as an accusation, more so than a question as Reno approached the big Sioux.

Backing up in superstitious horror, the red Hercules vanished into the receding ebb of aboriginals as they were driven from the summit.

The 300 plus defenders maintained the advantage of position; it was precarious and could only be saved by coming of night. Oceans of bare footed supermen ascended the hill like the enormous tidal surge accompanying a hurricane. Arapahos dismounted from their painted ponies to fill in gaps opened up by the shattering revolver fire. Literally everyone in Reno's command was using a Colt revolver. A wounded captain was seated in the open, prying swollen copper cartridge casings from the useless Springfields and reloading them.

As dusk approached, a light drizzle began to fall, and after a short while, stopped. The seething red masses had ebbed back to the giant village on the other side of the Little Bighorn and a few thousand warriors remained hidden about the surrounding hills, maintaining a desultory suppressive fire. Dead horses were moved into position in front of shallow rifle pits. Tens of thousands of flies swarmed each carcass, and would alight from the dead animal in a cloud each time one was moved. Wounded horses were put out of their misery and added to the defensive breastworks while wounded men screamed for water.

Small parties of men were sent on death missions to fill canteens at the river, only to be shot off their feet by thousands of rounds. Benteen's men used knives, spoons-whatever they on hand, to try to excavate rifle pits. The thundering war drums from the Indian camp reverberated through the valleys of the Little Bighorn River valley.

"Damn my soul!" expostulated the gnomely Captain Benteen, looking down from the hill, into the village through his binoculars, "They are set to burn them alive!"

Tied about the trunk of a large, solitary cottonwood were three captured soldiers, dry branches and brambles had been heaped around the base of the tree, and added to that were many tree branches and other flammables. The soldiers stood atop the ground cordwood stacked to waist level. The soldiers were secured tightly to the doomed tree with loops of thick hemp cordage. Shining with sweat, shirtless Indian women tended coal beds near the cottonwood tree, occasionally picking up coals with a shovel, and turning them over. Their breasts swayed and jiggled with each turn of the spade. The coals glowed from red to bright orange as a light breeze fanned them.

"Hey!" shouted one of the soldiers, "Do you speak English? Listen, we can help! Don't burn us and we'll give you the plans-tell you everything you want to know! Get your chief over here!"

The soldiers within eye view of the shiny, oiled women watched with horror piqued curiosity as the women, nude but for a loin cloth, stepped onto, and then walked across the coals. One of the women was completely naked-a tall Sioux who danced slowly atop a coal bed, raising one leg, and then the other while doing a balancing act. While doing this, she ran her hands through and lifted her shiny black shoulder length hair high above her head, and began gyrating her chest wildly; making her apple sized breasts swing violently back and forth. Sweat flew from her breasts and hissed as it landed on the glowing coals.

"I no speak the English, soldier," answered one of the raven haired beauties, leaning forward and against the hickory handle of the shovel, "an' I don't get no chief over here neither!" she laughed, as she resumed the shovel work.

Other bonfires burned, and hundreds of warriors danced about them, as calloused hands beat painted rawhide war drums. Many of these drums were painted in the colors of the Lakota four directions. Old men pranced about singing through toothless maws and banging war clubs against shields made of elk rawhide wrapped in rawhide lacing. They were decorated with images in black and red ochre paint. There were foot races, wrestling and great festivities all through the massive encampment.

Here and there captured cavalrymen were flayed alive while children who watched shrieked with glee. Groups of painted braves drank whiskey and looked hungrily up toward the moonlit hill where the remnants of the 7th cavalry were marooned.

Benteen and Reno watched the Roman holiday atmosphere in the camp through binoculars. Reno moved the glasses nearer and farther from his eyes to bring the imagery into sharper contrast, seeing several naked women, rather barbaric, Reno thought, setting fire to the wood kindling at the base of the cottonwood tree where the three soldiers stood tied. He saw the men lifting their heads to the sky and opening their mouths, but the thrum of hundreds of drums drowned the screams of the roasting men.

"If they come at us again tomorrow as they did today, the outcome is problematical." said Reno in a low voice to Benteen, who continued to watch the celebration.

"And?" queried the captain.

"The wounded. We cannot take them with us." Benteen lowered the binoculars and faced Reno.

"Now you listen here, and you listen to me good, Major Reno. We will not abandon this position on this night and were we to; we would not leave our wounded to the fate of those miserable souls below."

Reno moved in closer to Benteen, lowering his voice in a conspirational whisper.

"Be reasonable, Captain. The Indians are occupied, and now is our chance to evacuate this mound-a chance like this will not again present itself!"

An answer in the form of a sharp cuff across the face was Benteen's reply.

"Damned coward!" shouted Benteen.

"No and no! We cannot leave this mound on account of the wounded!" Benteen grabbed Reno by the cheeks using both hands, "and if you mutter such a suggestion again, I'll rip your eyes out!" again Benteen struck the major across the face, prompting Reno to step back, holding his mouth, again Benteen approached him and slapped him repeatedly. The Major receded into the darkness, his figure dimly visible in the wash of light from the countless Indian campfires which burned on the other side of the Little Bighorn River.

Captain Benteen again turned to the celebrations below and placed the binoculars to his eyes once more. Scanning the outside of the perimeter for movement, he made slow, broad sweeps with the binoculars, which amplified the light of the moon and the wavering light of the bonfires in the Indian camp. He saw movement at the edge of the camp...

A shot rang out, followed by dozens more as Jackson and Gerard lay flattened against the dew drenched grass.

"Hold your fire! Don't shoot! It's friendlies, Jackson and Gerard!" Jackson screamed at the top of his lungs.

"Hold your fire!" was repeated along both sides of the line and then the command was issued to advance to the line, a contact man was sent out to guide them into the hill's defenses. Benteen interviewed the men at length, discovering that there were more survivors in the woods on the other side of the river, including 1st Lt. DeRudio, "Count no Account" as Benteen acidly referred to him.

At a distance, lying in the prone position and using freshly excavated dirt on which to rest his binoculars, Major Reno watched his men writhe horribly as the flames took to the dried wood, he also watched the wild gesticulations and leaps of the tall Sioux woman who danced naked in front of the burning men. As their clothes burned from their bodies they saw her naked sweating form bending over, her back to them, she peered at them from between her legs, her long hair touching the coals and igniting.

« Chapter Eighteen »

THE SOIL FLOOR ON which Sitting Bull lay was not the soil endemic to the area; it had come from far away, when the oceans were lower and the coastlines different. In those days his ancestors had crossed a land mass that linked Alaska to Siberia. The soil was sacred soil, saturated in the ashes of long forgotten shamans, shamans who intermediated spiritually with the Holy Man who lay upon the sacred bed of soil. The face of the prostrated man was shiny with sweat; his eyes were rolled back revealing only the white sclera. The scarred face, ravaged from small pox was contorted into a grimace of agony, the lips pulled back and relaxed as he muttered incantations in a forgotten tongue, of a language dead for countless eons.

His spirit was on another astral plane, he was in total darkness, when a female voice answered him in his native tongue.

"You call, I come. For what deed do you seek to task Witkokaga? Why have you brought me through the vastness of time?"

The holy man could see nothing but darkness, he could not discern if he were still supine or standing. He could not tell up from down, he had the sensation of floating.

"Your people need a great service of you, Princess."

There was venom in the voice that responded to Sitting Bull.

"My people are long disappeared from the places you travel. We reside in another world from where you have torn me. Tell me what you want from me before I blast your soul!"

Sitting Bull was not perturbed; he had spoken to demons in wishing wells, to animals that answered and to men skinned alive whose tongues had been ripped from their mouths and through which spirits spoke.

"I beseech you to take the form of Mo-nah-se-tah." The tone of his voice was soft, and affectionate-it seemed to go unnoticed by Witkokaga, who sneered at the request, "Then you will give me Yellow Bird!"

Sitting Bull did not want to relinquish Yellow Bird, a potential hostage of great value in negotiations with the Yellow Hair if the Indians were not to win the coming battle.

"What do you see?" sneered the goddess.

"Blackness, Witkokaga, only the night." responded Sitting Bull.

Sitting Bull had the impression that his nose was bleeding, and that one side of his face had been pushed in, as from a sharp blow, but there was no sensation of pain. The voice of the goddess was like that of chimes tinkling on a cold arctic wind when she countered with hostility:

"What do you see?"

Suddenly he was blinded by a light of such intensity that he threw his hands to his face to shield his eyes. He peered through between his fingers at the deity which stood before him. Before him stood Mo-nah-se-tah. He could not disguise the surprise in his voice.

"Mo-nah-se-tah!" he cried.

"You look upon Witkokaga, High Priest! I am Witkokaga the Befooler!" came the spirit's reply, almost in the form of a retaliation.

The voice of Sitting Bull was soft, almost a whisper. His tongue caressed the Befooler with a cooing inflection. He spoke to her as though he were her lover.

"I implore you to deceive the one they call the Yellow Hair. I can see only a small distance into the future. They will come across water, but I don't know where."

Witkokaga approached the medicine man, she smelled of honeysuckle, he thought. Her eyes were dark pools that flooded into his mind.

"You hesitate to give me Yellow Bird!" she stabbed the words at the medicine man.

"He is of great value to me. The Yellow Hair does not know his son is among those he means to kill." responded Sitting Bull carefully, seductively.

The voice of Witkokaga softened, "You will give him to me."

"Yes, Witkokaga, the Yellow Hair's son is yours." responded the seer, albeit with a tone of remorse in his voice.

The goddess placed both hands on either side of the pockmarked face of Sitting Bull and issued a command to him.

"Then sleep, Sitting Bull, sleep and dream of me."

A litany of horrific screams issued from the tepee of the wizard as he dreamed. Sioux maidens, naked and shining with sweat bathed Sitting Bull's face with dampened cloths as he screamed.

"Nooooooo! Witkokaga! Noooooo!" The maidens looked about with fear, but saw only the twisting, writhing Sitting Bull who could not be wakened from his dream.

« Chapter Nineteen »

CUSTER HAD LOW crawled with his company commanders and spied upon the enormous Indian village from atop a summit of one of the nearby rolling hills. Behind him his exhausted troopers were fueled by adrenaline as they anticipated the coming fight, their horses panted from thirst. What the officers beheld boggled the imagination; the encampment stretched for miles.

"We'll ford the river where you see the ripples, the water is shallowest there. See that Indian woman bathing in the center of the river? The water is barely to the woman's belly, but we will have to be quick about it." spoke Custer, who scanned the river and then the camp with DeRudio's binoculars.

The commanding officer was met with silence as his captains surveyed the objective with disbelief.

"We will go across on line," Custer continued, "and then split up as previously arranged. Any of the braves not napping are being slain by Reno right now. Remember, the whole idea is to grab hostages, and then the surviving warriors will surrender to us."

The companies of cavalry filed rapidly from behind the bluffs in company formation, riding several abreast before halting and facing the river. Custer looked to his right and left, seeing the guidons which indicated the companies were in place.

I have total surprise! thought Custer.

He sat ramrod straight in his saddle and then stood up in the stirrups and turned around, looking directly behind him to make sure that Kellogg was nearby; he wanted the press reporter close at hand.

Now is the time! thought the Boy General. He took off his wide brimmed straw hat and waved it, while continuing to stand in the stirrups.

"We've run the buck to cover!" expostulated Custer, "Sound the charge!"

As Custer entered midway into the Little Bighorn River, a woman emerged from the water. Her appearance was incongruous with the situation.

"Belay that order! Mo-nah-se-tah! How did you appear? My son! Is he in this village?" the general was wild eyed and the words came from his mouth in a rush.

Custer was confused and uncertain. He was suddenly rocked with an emotion which was alien to him. He felt stark terror at risking the lives of his Indian wife and child. He considered calling off the attack altogether; he faced his dilemma with incertitude. The wings of cavalry on either side of him had stopped in midstream, as the rear echelons of cavalry came up behind, they stopped at the edge of the stream.

Shouting could be heard from the Indian camp, braves were running toward them-at first dozens, then hundreds. Some would stop and shoot from the shoulder at the soldiers, while others ran past them, war whooping with bloodlust.

In the autumn of 1868, Custer had led the 7th Cavalry in an attack on a Cheyenne village led by Chief Black Kettle. Among the killed was Chief Little Rock, Mo-nah-se-tah's father. That fact did not stop the former general from marrying the 17 year old beauty and taking her as his second wife.

When Elizabeth Custer arrived and caught onto the liaison, she made the striking beauty take the infant and leave. Since Elizabeth had no desire to have marital relations with the man who had sterilized her, she condoned his philandering. Extramarital affairs conducted discreetly were one thing, but open marriage to a second wife was intolerable. Pitifully, as Mo-nah-se-tah left the military post, she offered the infant to the childless couple. Libbie was generous and let Custer make the choice. The embarrassment of having an illegitimate Indian child by a Cheyenne wife would destroy his bid for the Presidency, and so he watched his family go.

"For the love of God, Mo-nah-se-tah, mount my horse!" commanded Custer as he leaned over, stretching his arm out to his wife.

She stepped forward, her lips pulled tightly back in a bestial sneer. She growled deeply at the confused general, who was frozen in horror at what he was seeing.

"I am the spirit that deceives fools!" She began laughing and as her peals of cold, rude laughter froze his blood, he saw her become diaphanous and vanish.

His officers had seen their commanding officer speaking to the woman in the water, and were stunned at the incident. As the volume of fire from the Indian village intensified, they implored him to come to his senses. From behind a rock on the opposite side of the river, a brave named White Cow Bull took aim with his Henry at a figure wearing a buckskin jacket and wide brimmed hat...

Custer was hit low in the left side of the chest, the bullet narrowly missing the heart but passing through one lung and entering into the other. The energy imparted from the large, slow moving .44 caliber 300 grain lead slug unseated the commander from his mount, and he fell into the river. Instantly the attack faltered, and uncertainty flooded the ranks as they saw their commander helped back onto his saddle, where he slumped in a heap. The guidon bearer was shot off his mount, as was the next man who attempted to recover the standard. As Custer was escorted to the rear, toward the highest hill, a skirmisher's line was rapidly formed, with every fourth man taking four horses, as the balance of the cavalry fought on foot against a rapidly growing tidal wave of howling warriors that began to wash over them.

Custer's entourage rushed him up the steep slope leading to the ridge as he leaned forward, arms around the neck of Vic, his mount, as he tried to breathe and maintain consciousness.

"Mo-nah-se-tah!" he gurgled over and over.

Realization came to him in a flood as he saw that his future was at an end. He knew he was dying and knew that all of his descendants would be from his Cheyenne wife, Mo-nah-se-tah.

"Oh please forgive me, God!" he prayed, "Give me one more chance!"

Guilt washed over him for having spurned his infant son, who was now an outcast among every tribe and nation that he traveled to with his mother. Vic seemed to know intuitively where to go as the small nucleus of command headed up the slope of the ridge.

"I think not of Libbie in my last minutes, but of Mo-nah-se-tah!"

The ridge was about a half a mile in length, and punctuated with several knolls. It offered a sweeping panorama of the Montana Territory in all directions. To the west was a vast ocean of prairie, to the east was a labyrinth of gulches covered with buffalo grass, wild plum trees, and sagebrush. The command elements for the most part were with this group, and they took their crippled leader to the north end-the highest knoll. Quickly they began setting up skirmishers, but before they could consolidate the circumference of the knoll, they were taken under fire by Gall, a Hunkpapa Lakota Chief standing well over six feet tall and weighing nearly 300 pounds, whose hordes had attained the summit of the knoll.

If things couldn't get any worse, the trailing companies had been heavily engaged on three sides as they tried to reach the command element. Ultimately, they were engulfed and established impromptu defenses on the southern knoll and a dip on the reverse slope several hundred yards back, where they were in effect islands in a seething red sea. Of these three islands, the one on the south end was the strongest, desperately defended by Custer's brother-in-law, 1st Lt James Calhoun.

Some of the troopers in Company E whose horses had been shot out from under them made a mad dash for a deep gulch, seeking cover; they were overtaken by Cheyenne, led by Lame White Man, who grabbed Associated Press Reporter Mark Kellogg by the back of the collar. Lame White Man jerked Kellogg back and halted his retreat toward the sanctuary of the deep ravine.

Furious hand to hand fighting ensued-the soldiers shooting their .45s into washboard etched stomachs and meat loafed chests before using the big Colts as clubs.

Kellogg, a slightly built man of 45 years with thinning grey hair over a high forehead, moved adroitly to the side as Lame White Man slashed at his head, taking off his right ear. His spectacles were perched atop a Pinocchio nose and were smeared with sweat; they rested askew minus the supporting ear. His shallow face was offset by a thick set of sideburns, blood and sweat flew in droplets from them as he ducked and weaved while trying to dodge the murderous slashes of Lame White Man's Bowie knife.

"Listen!" shouted Kellogg at his attacker, "you don't have to do this!"

"Pig!" retorted the obsessed Cheyenne chief, who was making jabs and slashing movements with the knife as he advanced on the reporter in increments, "I mean to gut you like a pig!"

Kellogg locked eyes with the big Cheyenne, who wielded the Bowie knife with murderous skill. Even in this desperate situation, Kellogg noted with a reporter's attention to detail that the opponent he faced wore a thin, pronounced moustache, meticulously manicured. Lame White Man drove the big knife into Kellogg's pigeon chest with sledgehammer force, impaling it into Kellogg's shorthand notebook.

"Bastard!" growled Lame White Man like a wolf, as he tried to extract the large fighting knife, designed by the controversial duelist and frontiersman, Jim Bowie.

Lame White Man had pronounced Caucasoid features; his head was dolichocephalic and reflected the features of his captive white mother very strongly. The soft hazel irises could not belie the bestial fury that raged out of control inside them.

Kellogg's fear was overridden with passion to live as he fumbled for, found, and wielded his needle sharp pencil like a stiletto. Grasping the pencil with his right hand, he drove it full force into the left eye of Lame White Man, who turned his head violently aside, breaking off the pencil in his eye socket.

"Aaaaargh!" shouted Lame White Man, "My eye!"

Kellogg was frozen in horror as he watched the Cheyenne war chief try to extract the writing instrument from the sclera; the pencil had embedded into the orbit of the skull, penetrating the maniac's brain. The half blinded aboriginal bellowed like a blinded Cyclops.

"You little shit!" screamed the enraged Cheyenne, "I'm going to rip your throat out with my bare hands!"

The big chief withdrew his hands from his ruined eye and advanced on Kellogg with hellish intent, ham like hands opening and closing. Kellogg's gaze was fixed on the remaining eye of the older Cheyenne warrior, an eye that beamed antipathy from its dilated pupil. The greased hair was parted in the middle and dangled in the form of two large braids on either side, these swung back and forth as he shook his head in rage and pain.

Kellogg pulled Lame White Man's Bowie knife from his shirt; the note pad was still imbedded on the murderous blade tip. The tip of the knife had punctured an inch through the ledger, leaving a deep puncture in the string reporter's bony chest. Quickly, violently, Kellogg swung the heavy knife down on Lame White Man's head.

"Haaaaaaaa!!!" screamed Kellogg as he swung the oversized fighting knife in an arcing motion.

The knife struck with the effect of a meat cleaver, splitting Lame White Man's head down to the high set cheek bones, the blade had cleaved cleanly between the two hemispheres of the brain. The paper notebook pad had dislodged itself from the tip of the knife when the blade rent through the cranial bone, its leaves of paper catching and flying in the gusty wind. The square set jaw of the gigantic Cheyenne opened in a deafening scream as he locked his hands around Kellogg's skinny neck and began to throttle him.

"Die! Funny little man!" growled Lame White Man as his thumbs dug into and worked their way into the trachea of Mark Kellogg, who tried ineffectually to break the grip of the maddened chief.

The 250 pound dynamo of raw strength hurled himself onto the ectomorphic form of the desperate string reporter, slamming him onto the hard, dry ground. The veins in Kellogg's neck distended into large vessels the size of rope as Kellogg struggled to break the grip, twisting his head from side to side as he did so, the back of his head was gouged by small sharp rocks with the twisting motion.

"Let go!" gasped Kellogg who saw the visage of his antagonist blur as he lost consciousness.

Nearly all of the dismounted soldiers were dead, the few survivors were being shot in the deep coulee. A warrior rushed to help the chief, but took a stray bullet and crumpled to the ground. Lame White Man released the broken, distended neck of the newspaper reporter, and leaning forward, bit deeply into the pronounced Adam's apple of the deceased Kellogg. The Bowie knife that was still wedged in his skull impeded his efforts; the wooden handle that was fastened onto the tang with brass studs retarded his progress. Standing up, he looked at his fellow braves, and spat out the Adam's apple. He took two steps while wiping the gore from his mouth with the back of a forearm corded with steel cable muscle. Then he collapsed as he tried to remove the overbuilt blade, the handle of which he grasped with both hands as hundreds of fine threads of blood sprayed several feet into the air from all around the deeply imbedded blade.

Six hundred yards northward on the ridge was another island, where the terrain dipped. This was defended by the men of Company I, and commanded by the hard drinking Irishman Captain Myles Keogh. Keogh had a reputation as a lady's man and a stern officer, he carried a cane with a wolf's head made of silver. Often he would cane his men for minor infractions during in ranks inspections, and he was despised by them. They despised him because he was a Catholic, an Irishman, an officer, and a bully.

The high, shrill sounds of war flutes drifted through the cacophony of noise, as the screams of wounded horses mingled with the war whoops of charging Sioux and Cheyenne.

"Hold your bloody positions!" screamed the big captain in his Irish brogue. The hulking Irishman saw clearly that Calhoun's position was being overwhelmed; Calhoun was waddling like a porcupine with dozens of arrows protruding from him as he fired his Colt point blank into the screaming mouth of a Cro-Magnon like warrior.

"We're gonna havta make a run for the high knoll! Over there where Custer is!" screamed Keogh as he looked back over his shoulder to the knoll at the end of the ridge where Custer's guidons were snapping smartly in the wind.

There were several thousand natives armed with a mismatched assortment of lances, flint lock pistols, muzzle loading rifles and repeaters crawling through the tall buffalo grass toward them, these men were between Keogh and Custer's hill. Slapping his horse Comanche on the rear with his cane, he sent the big gelding into the grasses and ordered his men to follow the horse, while he remained covering the rear.

"Follow my horse! Every man for himself! Get after it while I cover you!" shouted the Irishman at the top of his lungs.

The remnants of his company broke and ran for the distant promontory as Keogh resumed firing with two Colt revolvers. He saw waves of Indian bowmen further down the slope; they were loosing shafts in an upward trajectory as they walked, not taking aim, and not seeking cover. The effect of the plunging fire could not be overstated as the arrows plunged into soldiers who had taken cover behind fallen horses.

At this moment Crazy Horse, the orchestrator of General Crook's defeat at the Battle of Rosebud Creek, entered the fray. With an entourage of several hundred warriors he crashed into the fleeing soldiers, who began dropping their rifles, while others began shooting themselves in the head with their revolvers. One soldier, a grizzled Civil War veteran, took aim a Keogh's leg with his revolver and blew the captain's knee off.

"To the devil with you, you damned Mick!" he shouted at the officer.

Wheeling about like a dervish, he shot twice into a clump of a dozen advancing braves, knocking two of them back. In seconds five of them were on him, but he'd saved the last bullet for himself. Cursing and spitting tobacco juice at being denied a captive, they turned their fury on Keogh, who stuck the muzzle of his revolver in his mouth and blew the top of his head off before they could stop him.

"Take my bulldogs, Tom!" Gasped the dying general. "I'm giving you the command! Try to save what you can!" Thomas Custer surveyed the situation with horror.

156

"There is nothing left to save, Audie! You've got your derringer, use it!" The Custer elements never had time to form up as a whole, as had Reno's. Instead it had to stop and fight as it was overtaken, the already tiny unit being subdivided into three smaller entities. The sound of gunfire was deafening, and Thomas Custer never heard the shot that his brother put through the side of his head.

The bloodshot onyx eyes of Rain In The Face saw the lone officer standing among the clumps of dead horses and soldiers whose rifles would not fire. Bloodshot eyes which beheld the object of a grudge, and the eyes narrowed into slits as the brain behind them fomented a way to skirt around and behind the figure. The figure's eyes locked with his own and recognition was there, amplifying the horror of the standing soldier's predicament.

The handsome features of the brave were distorted by a fierce grimace of hate, hate of having endured the most humiliating of any insult a Sioux warrior could suffer. The greased hair was parted in the middle and woven tightly into two braids which descended below the swell of the pectorals. The braids were held intact with rawhide and colored cloth. The high forehead was atop an aquiline face reminiscent of a Trojan; a Sioux Hector, only the epicanthic folds above his eyes differentiated his regal visage from that of the Mediterranean races. A double bandolier of ammunition for his Winchester crisscrossed the heavy slabs of pectoral muscles which played with each arm movement. A gun belt with its holstered .44 Remington revolver was slung at an angle on his narrow loins. He wore a loin cloth of heavy red fabric over a set of elk skin leather breeches. Rather than moccasins, he wore sandals in the Mexican fashion.

Rain In The Face had murdered the fort's dentist in cold blood, and had drunkenly boasted of the deed at an Indian gathering outside the fort's main sultry store. Word had gotten back to Thomas Custer, who arrested the brave and had him shackled in irons with a white ne'er do well for about a year, pending a death sentence. Through the winter with nothing but a single blanket and with snow blowing through the log spacings, Rain In The Face had survived on hatred. Chaining a Sioux warrior to a white man and locking him in a shack was the worst insult that could be given a Sioux, and Rain In The Face vowed revenge.

Suddenly everything went white, with stars flying in all directions as Tom fell forward face first onto the ground. An Indian coup stick was rising and falling, rising and falling.

Rain In The Face smashed the sternum with the large rock and took his boning knife-a wicked bone handled instrument with a four inch blade, and cut through the broken bones of the younger Custer's chest, cut through and reached into the chest cavity, grabbing the yet beating heart with his right hand while severing the great vessels and arteries with the knife held in his left hand.

Kneeling on both knees over the lifeless body, Rain In The Face held the beating heart up high over his forehead and toward the sun. Then he began to rip and tear at the tough fibrous cardiac muscle with his strong tobacco stained teeth. The beaten armbands of copper pressed into the skin as the bulging biceps strained against them. Holding a quivering shred of the tough muscle in his mouth, he spat it full into the flattened remains of Thomas's face. The heart continued to expand and contract as he bit into the right atrium, causing blood to spurt across his eyes, temporarily blinding him.

The smell and coppery taste of the hot blood overcame the Hunkpapa's self-control and he began ripping and tearing at the throbbing double pump, shredding it with his strong teeth and swallowing chunks of it without chewing. He held the ravished heart to his mouth with both hands as he rended the muscle, and a deep growl issued from the blood masked mouth. Swallowing the quivering hunks of raw heart muscle whole, he paused for breath. He could feel the separate vestiges of the heart moving in his stomach, as though it had a power of its own, and he renewed his rending of the heart remnants. He was growling and slavering like a rabid wolf as he tore at the flesh. Suddenly, without warning, he felt a sudden energy-a vitality borne of the warrior's heart he had just eaten. Rain In The Face stood up, and roared like a mountain lion, causing the warriors nearest him to step back in terror.

« Chapter Twenty »

"Wake up! Wake up Mrs. Custer!" spoke the Indian maid servant in a commanding tone.

"Get up! You have to eat and get dressed. Big fighting in creek today for Poquerhienee."

It was with difficulty that Libbie roused from the deep slumber, early as it was. Not yet four thirty in the morning.

"Get up! Get up! Elizabeth Custer!"

Then she felt the covers pulled suddenly from her, and the icy night air of the open windowed bedroom startled her awake.

The throng of spectators had gathered along either side of the creek bank and were for the most part members of the various tribes of Cree who supplied scouts and assisted with work details of Fort Abraham Lincoln. Entire sides of antelope roasted over glowing coals of cooking fires while hot coffee brewed and Indian men passed bottled whiskey from mouth to mouth. Naked children frolicked in the water as their mothers commingled with each other spreading the family's gossip. Everyone was oblivious to the struggle playing out a thousand miles away as they sang, talked, played and anticipated the coming contest between the two young contenders for the chance to suckle the breasts of the vivacious Poquerhienee.

"Must the children always run about naked?" complained the uncomfortable Margaret, turning her head from Libbie and seeing the elderly sachem of the reservation.

He was relieving himself on the side of a large cottonwood tree twenty feet away. He spat tobacco juice and smiled at her as he shook the droplets of urine from his uncircumcised member.

"Libbie, I feel inclined to vomit!"

"Shhhh! Now, Margie! Listen to the drums and whistles; Poquerhienee is exiting her tepee this selfsame moment! She is by rite required to witness the competition, because she elected that they fight for her."

A cloud of grasshoppers took flight as Poquerhienee walked barefoot to the creek's edge, and sat down

161

cross legged on a quilted blanket beneath the shade of a stout cotton wood tree, which emitted a small shower of white dander with each gust of hot wind. Some of the white windfall alighted on the raven black hair of the sanguine beauty, which had been brushed straight and fell over her slender shoulders. Atop the narrow shoulders was a gazelle neck and to this was a head that bore the face of primordial beauty.

The forehead was sloped slightly back and the eyebrows were plucked. The eyes were dark coals, set closely together and bisected by a nose ridge that started high. The ridge descended at an even angle into a petulant, petite nose, whose nostrils flared slightly at the scent of roasting antelope. The lips were full, darkly pigmented and rested nicely above a perfectly formed chin. The cheeks were high set, but not overly so, and she had a somewhat Aztec appearance, large hoop earrings depended from either ear lobe. She was not heavily breasted, but her hips were amply formed, and the snugly fitting dress of buckskin did not hide her luscious curvature.

Her dress was adorned with religious imagery and studded with brass. Around her neck draped necklaces of beads and bear claws. She wore bracelets of beaten copper and rings of gold and silver acquired as gifts. She smiled, revealing teeth white as ivory as other women and younger girls sat and kneeled beside her, wishing her a long and productive marriage. Her two champions remained in their tepees with their supporters, their gods, and their hopes and dreams. They spoke incantations and painted themselves with magical designs to give them strength in the fight to come.

Margaret sipped a cooling drink as she fanned herself. Gnats and blue bottle flies were a constant nuisance, as well as the painful bite of the ubiquitous horsefly. She had removed her white sunhat and unbuttoned her blouse as far as modesty would allow. The cleavage of her sweaty breasts showed prominently as she set down the drink and fanned herself more vigorously.

"Well!" expostulated Margaret Custer Calhoun, "I have to say that Poquerhienee displays a fine countenance."

Libbie sat on a folding field chair, she wore a broad white sun hat, underneath which her hair was tightly spun into a bun. She wore a white short sleeved blouse unbuttoned to the breast line and a gray riding dress. Her boots sat atop the bed sheet which covered the ground where the two sisters in law sat.

"Do you imagine Poquerhienee removing her animal skins boldly in a private audience for you?" asked Libbie, there was a cruel teasing tone inflected into her melodic voice.

Also present was the barely perceptible trace of jealousy in the melodical tenor of Libbie's ensconced barb. Quickly the tone changed as Libbie followed the question with one of her redundant, philosophical expostulations. Already the author of several bestselling books, she always tried to speak in prosaic form.

"We will remember this pleasurable day as imbued in a tint that compounds myriad hues and colors into a pastel of rainbow. It would be impossible to subtract one single flavor of color so perfectly aligned and explain how its singularity paints the cavalcade of colors. The day promises to be long and clear, in the stead of soaring buildings and traveled streets, we have lofty clouds and gurgling streams. Happiness is readily categorized into the immediate needs and fulfilments in this wondrous abode." expostulated the ebullient Libbie Custer.

Libbie continued to fan herself with one of the coveted folding fans, decorated with the artistic drawings of the Japanese language.

If I could but articulate my thoughts in such an eloquent way as you, thought Margaret to herself, as she was momentarily hypnotized by the motion of Elizabeth's fan.

Libbie waved the fan back and forth slowly, creating an airflow that cooled the skin of her partially exposed chest. The fan was shaped like the sector of a circle and made of thin paper mounted on slats that revolved around a fulcrum so that it could be closed when not in use.

"Oh Libbie, you have such a way with words." murmured the recalcitrant Margaret, "You know I only have eyes for you."

"Perhaps so, Margie, but you are one with developed appreciation for beauty, only ladies of culture and distinction can appreciate the inherent beauty of the female form. To see the bold admiration of your eyes while I am in my most naked state makes my heart palpitate. You may imagine how Poquerhienee appears absent her raiment, but she prefers the obscene vulgarity of male anatomy, and will never aspire to our cultural refinement.

"Often," Libbie continued, "I would leave my door boldly open while I undressed, knowing that you watched surreptitiously from your bed across the hall, feigning sleep. How impatiently I awaited the diminution of your temerity,"

"Libbie, I would spy upon you through the keyhole of the doorknob when you came to visit!" confided Margaret.

"I know. From the very first time I was a guest at your father's home, I knew you were spying through the keyhole, and I knew the moment would come when my mechanizations saw fruition and you timidly would implore me undress openly to your audience. But I knew that the timidity was a façade – a veneer behind which was developing a lady of the highest estheticism possible." responded Libbie to Margaret, there as a tone of approval in the tenor of her voice.

The fantasy of being present while Poquerhienee undressed had infused Margaret with a vigor that surprised her, and she stood abruptly from the field chair when she espied the first contestant stepping forward out of the opening of the buffalo skin tepee.

The tepee was one of the large ones; a conical structure standing about twenty feet high, owing to the fact that it was in this case, a semi- permanent structure immediately outside the fort. This large dwelling was constructed of four redwood lodge poles tied at the top using rawhide and pegs. The poles flared out at the base, and around it were tanned buffalo hides stitched together with rawhide thong, this formed a sheath that kept the structure cool in the summer and warm in the winter. At the top were two adjustable smoke flaps, from which arose a wisp of smoke from a small fire within. The tepee was decorated with many drawings of celestial objects, horses, and the warrior's deeds in battle. Tufts of buffalo hair, dyed porcupine quills and beads also adorned the outside of the structure. The warrior had to stoop to exit the four foot doorway that had been cut into the hide.

"Oh, look, Margie! What a grotesque example of our Indian allies! Look at how tall and well-proportioned he is! His body could have been sculpted by Michelangelo!" ejaculated the exuberant Libbie in a jocular manner of expression.

The resemblance to the David of which Libbie had alluded was not lost on the watchful eye of Margaret. However much the resemblance to Michelangelo's David may have been, it stopped at the neck and in no way could have been compared to the hatchet-like face and sneering mouth, the lips of which were pulled back to reveal teeth sharpened to points. The teeth, stained brown by a lifetime of chewing tobacco reminded Margaret of the nightmarish man ogres in the bedtime stories her mother would read to her during childhood.

This hideous man stood by the creek side, flexing his muscles and limbering up. His magnificent tattoos stood out on his glistening brown skin, heavily oiled in bear grease to make his opponent's grasp all the more difficult. He gazed at the oblivious Poquerhienee fifty feet away, who pretended to ignore him as she laughed and talked with her female friends. Teeth That Rip Flesh spat green tinged phlegm into the sluggishly moving water and watched as dozens of small fish struck at and fought over it, until it was gone and they had vanished into their fairy haunts in the crystal clear water.

Teeth That Rip Flesh looked at the image that reflected up at him; head shaven to deny his opponent purchase, a large scar from a knife fight that began at where his hairline would have been and extended at an angle horizontally down his sloped forehead, across his right eye and terminating at his jawline beneath his earlobe. Although he could discern light and movement with the ruined eye, images appeared blurry and he was for the most part blind in it. Both ears had been largely bitten off in previous hand to hand combats and only vestigial cartilage remained of the outer auditory organs.

The tall, muscular warrior's mouth was tattooed with short, blue vertical dashes, the lips were permanently stained blue and the chin was tattooed with a series of bold, black vertical strokes. The body was adorned from the shoulders down in intricate hieroglyphically designed patterns, the skin having been traumatized by sharpened objects such as knives, needle awls, and flints. The pigments consisted of compounds including plant dyes extracted from nuts and berries, along with ground up minerals. The tattoos that covered the massively built Arikawa invoked magical strength and protection, having been carefully imbued into the man's skin by an old wizard, inside a tepee that covered an ancient well from which he invoked the names of horrific gods.

"He certainly has the appearance of a ruthless competitor, Libbie!" Margaret said to her sister in law as she shuddered at the pagan visage that sang a prayer to his unnamable gods.

From a similar tepee on the opposite side of the creek emerged Pretty Man; a man of about twenty years, perhaps fifteen years younger than the brute he opposed. Although similar in height and build, their appearance could not have been more diametrically opposed. This Arikawa warrior had thick black hair, the hairline beginning low on the high set forehead, and was tightly braided into a single ponytail, secured with a band of rawhide. His aristocratic face bore an unscarred and Roman-like visage. He began stretching exercises as he limbered for the coming contest.

Pretty Man looked first at Poquerheinee, who lounged lazily with her entourage beneath the venerable cottonwood, which had shaded many a young maiden during these events. She ate blackberries from a porcelain bowl as she swatted at gnats and flies. The high pitched whirring of thousands of cicadas intermingled with the drums, flutes and singing. Added to the cacophony of eerie music were the scents of the cooking fires, fueled by a combination of dried wood and patties of dehydrated horse dung. Several small dogs had been spitted and were being roasted slowly over subdued, gray coal beds.

The cawing of crows that competed with turkey buzzards and countless mongrel dogs for refuse discarded onto the rubbish heap outside the fort was ignored by Pretty Man. Libbie and Margaret continued to fan themselves as Libbie intimated to Margie the background of the contest about to ensue.

"Behold the young Hercules as he stretches and limbers his muscles, Margaret. Juxtapose his image in your mind's eye against the tattooed leviathan that awaits him at the water's edge. Do you discern a likeness between the two red men?" questioned Elizabeth to her sister in law.

"Well, no, actually. The much older one appears as a hideous demon, while the younger is of a much more agreeable countenance, almost handsome if such can be said of an aboriginal man, or any man." answered Margaret.

Elizabeth Custer began laughing,

Margaret openly watched Libbie's breasts jiggle from the laughter and she was mentally aware of the cruelty intoned in the melodic expostulation. Libbie looked up at Margaret, who was still standing.

"They are close knit, Margaret!" she said, smiling, "It is the Native American dearest to me who intimated this random factor into the morbid equation of lust and passion! I must express my utmost gratitude unto my very best Native American friend, who most dearly adores me as I do her, Et-nah-wah-ruchta! Why, we were speaking intimately, as all close friends do, as she assisted me with my bath one day. Well! She told me that the combat was of a familial nature, peculiar to us perhaps, but not to our stalwart Native allies. These very same Hectors who unknowingly emulate the heroes that traversed the pages throughout the many great works of Classical Greece!"

Several dozen more braves rode up on ponies painted in ceremonial designs. These were in the form of circles and lightning bolts. Large red loops were painted in ochre around each eye, and solid dots adorned the flanks of each animal. Some of the braves brought their wives on horseback with them. Many of the men were drunk by now, on fort whiskey and warm, flat ale made from the seed of forage grasses that had been germinated, steamed, and allowed to ferment. This strong, foul tasting concoction was drunk from bowls made of wood and stoneware.

Small cast iron pots simmered with bird brain stew at the side of coal beds, while large caldrons of buffalo stew (also called tanka-me-a-lo) hung suspended over glowing embers, heavily flavored with wild onion, juniper berry, and cayenne peppers. Buffalo jerky was abundant. Strong, white teeth of children ripped and tore at it, while old toothless men and hags gummed with determined perseverance. Corn bread, acorn and fry breads were carefully tended in iron skillets atop rocks that contained the cooking embers. Steady dripping of fat from roasting antelope spitted on cottonwood saplings hissed as they fell on the glowing coals with the turning of the crank.

Some of the fat was captured and added to steaming pots of succotash. To the feast were additional delicacies of rabbit, raccoon, and opossum. Skillets filled with grasshoppers fried and popped in hissing pork lard. Cayenne pepper, ground to a powder was dusted over these and the crunchy locusts were hungrily devoured. Muscadines, blackberries and raspberries were on hand in prodigious quantities. Rock hard Indian corn of myriad colors softened in kettles of boiling water and succulent quail roasted on thin cottonwood branches held by hand over horse dung fueled flame.

A single long blast from an old, heavily dented bugle ushered a silence among the milling throng of revelers. The shirtless village sachem, a stoutly built man of six feet, with graying black hair and a ridiculous pair of oversized silver earrings began speaking. The heavy beer gut of the man swung back and forth as he paced about the foot of a large boulder, he paused in his oration in order to climb and stand atop it. Speaking in Arikawa, the tone of his voice was high pitched, with nasal inflections.

Quite drunk, he tottered while he spoke. Et-nah-wah-ruchta translated the sachem's oratory to the two officer's wives as best she could.

"Running Bull say two esteemed warrior vie for breasts of Poquerhienee."

The sachem's rotund belly, burned nearly black from doing nothing but fishing and drinking beer for sixteen hours a day was shiny with sweat. It was a reservoir of latent energy, full of explosive power.

"...say she choose make' em fight. Running Bull say..."

At that moment Running Bull lost his balance in mid-sentence and fell sideways off the uneven precipice of the thirty foot high boulder. He did not shout as he fell. Striking the ground face first, his head split open on a flat surfaced rock, like a watermelon. As several hundred tribesmen ran to their leader, Libbie and Margaret could not stifle their laughter, provoking an urgent warning from Et-nah-wah-ruchta to be silent. A fierce looking Cree emerged from the throng surrounding the sachem. He wore a ceremonial head bonnet of eagle feathers that extended down to the ground behind him. Casting a savage stare at Teeth That Rip Flesh and Pretty Man, then glowering at Poquerhienee, he shouted in his native tongue:

"Fight!"

Instantly the solemnness of the moment was lost, and the respected sachem lay forgotten by his tribe, but not forgotten by the hordes of blue bottle flies that already swarmed the massive skull injury.

Both men ran naked at full pace, their parts swinging wildly, and leapt into the chilled water.

The conundrum of the festivities was disrupted further by thunderous applause and cheering as the men disappeared beneath the water, swimming toward one another. Breast stroking and frog kicking underwater to add momentum to their speed.

"Libby, I have for the life of me never seen a sight more disgusting! The way that the uncircumcised members of these two hoodlums swung and slapped about as they made for the water almost made me retch!"

There was no sign of either combatant as Margaret spoke. Poquerhienee for the first time seemed to show interest as she scanned the water's surface for any sign of turbulence.

"Shhhh! Margie! Be cognizant of where we are presently stationed. We are guests here and privy to a special event. If you wish to watch Et-nah-wah-ruchta undress me tonight then you will be respectful of our Indian allies."

The crisp admonition of the older white woman to her younger in law was overheard with anger by the enraged Et-nah-wah-ruchta, who had intended on bedding with her husband soon as the victor entered the tent of Poquerhienee. Adding insult to injury was the fact that now Et-nah-wah-ruchta would have to perform for two of these strange white women, who seemed to detest men but preferred their own sex.

Suddenly an explosion erupted from the water as the two men porpoised up. One with an arm lock around the other's neck, both gasping for air in the chest deep water. Libby was startled by the sudden grasp of Et-nah-wah-ruchta's hand on her wrist, the strength of which frightened her. The black, heartless eyes of her Indian maid servant were transfixed on the struggle ensuing. Her other hand was clenched into a fist, shaking it with each shaking motion of the two combatants.

"Et-nah-wah-ruchta, let go, you're hurting me!" cried Elizabeth Custer, trying to pull away from the powerful grip of the Arikawa woman.

Margaret watched in alarm as Libbie began to writhe and twist in an attempt to extricate her wrist from the iron grip of Et-nah-wah-ruchta, who seemed hypnotized by the death struggle taking place fifty feet away in the creek.

Teeth That Rip Flesh struggled to maintain consciousness as his pulse pounded in his ears. The arm lock Pretty Man maintained was constricting the veins and arteries of his neck, as well as his windpipe. His eyes were open, and bulged out of their sockets in an obscene, bug eyed aspect. His naturally dark complexion was nearly blackened as the veins in his forehead stood out to the point of rupturing, and his face purpled to the shade of indigo. Without thinking, Teeth That Rip Flesh relinquished the grip on the arm-bar that crossed his throat, and using both hands seized the long ponytail braid of Pretty Man, and yanked it forward in an overhead motion with all of his strength.

The effect was game changing; the thickly braided ponytail, widely based at the scalp, tore loose in a long, ragged and uneven scalp lock. This, Teeth That Rip Flesh threw contemptuously into the water in front of him. Instead of maintaining his hold, Pretty Man relinquished his arm lock and grabbed with both hands at the top of his head, his fingers feeling only bone. The suture lines of the skull were clearly visible. He looked to the blue sky and began screaming so hard that no sound came from his mouth. Teeth That Rip Flesh waded several steps away with his back turned, rubbing his neck to restore circulation.

Poquerhienee up to now had effectively maintained a façade of disinterest in the melee occurring in the aqua arena. It had been her intention to see her younger suitor kill the cruel and abusive older man, who nevertheless owned several hundred horses and was continually away from the fort. But now her disinterest had been replaced not only with concern that her young heart throb might succumb to her other, more gruesome champion, but also the horror that she would endure being his wife. She stared at the horrific aberration of the horse trader struggling away from the panicked Pretty Man. As she watched him kneading the circulation back into the thick sinews of his neck, he locked eyes with her, and smiled.

Teeth That Rip Flesh turned around, sound roaring back into his ears as his senses restored. On both shorelines of the creek crowds milled about, waving and shouting drunkenly, firing rifles and revolvers into the air, urging the combatants on. But there was no sign of Pretty Man. Suddenly Teeth That Rip Flesh was lifted up from beneath the water, his knees held together as he fell backward and disappeared under the agitated surface.

"Look at what you've done to my arm!" Elizabeth Custer had the sleeve pulled up to her elbow; red welts were clearly visible from the firm grip of the excited Et-nah-wah-ruchta.

"I very sorry, Mrs. Custer. I dunno what come over me. I sorry. I watch fightin' in creek, like watchen'em fight. Please forgive."

Elizabeth noted absently that both of the fighters had gone underwater again and turned to the evilly beautiful Indian face that beseeched her with imploring, sloe eyes.

"Well, I suppose my forgiveness could have a price." answered Libbie, the tone of her voice hardening as she did so.

Poquerhienee's view of the combat was being obstructed by drunken revelers who had forgotten that she was the belle of the ball; they were jostling and pushing one another aside in order to get a better view of the struggle agitating the water. Shouting over the din of laughter and shouting, of curses and threats, of mothers screaming for their children to not enter the water too near where the two competitors fought, Poquerhienee gesticulated for several of her entourage to assist her onto the lower branches of the tree. She observed with dread the figures of the two struggling men as they periscoped up once more from the water, each with his hands clamped around the other's neck as they strangled each other. The corners of Poquerhienee's mouth were contorted into a snarling frown as she saw that the remaining scalp of Pretty Man had slid part way down the skull as he throttled the object of his antipathy. The temporal muscles on the sides of the skull were visible as his muscles bunched on his massive arms with the effort.

Teeth That Rip Flesh felt the thumbs of Pretty Man digging into his esophagus, and he redoubled his effort as he kneaded his dirty thumbnails into, and beneath the neck skin of Pretty Man. Once the thumb nails had cut through the skin, getting his thumbs under the skin and ripping it loose was his next order of business. The wounds were not life threatening, but they did cause Pretty Man to release his grip on the bull neck of Teeth That Rip Flesh. Reflexively Pretty Man thrust both hands to his own neck and Teeth That Rip Flesh reacted immediately; lunging forward and sinking his sharpened, pointed teeth into the massive trapezius muscle that extended out from the neck and onto the broad right shoulder. Then he ripped a mouth full of flesh from the steak like slab, swallowing it whole as he received an enormous eardrum bursting open handed cuff to the left ear.

"What price, what price you have Lady Custer?" Et-nah-wah-ruchta asked, with uneasy suspicion.

"Well, my sister by marriage has always found the male anatomy to be utterly repugnant, and while I allow for audience, I repudiate all forms of physical contact altogether. The touch of a hand to my person places into my disposition an utter state of melancholy."

The monologue was lost on the Indian woman.

"I wish those two pigs would hurry along and kill each other, Libbie." spoke Margaret, her voice was low and controlled.

A roar erupted from the crowds thronging either edge of the creek, distracting the trio and drawing the attention of Et-nah-wah-ruchta once more to the fighting in the water.

Teeth That Rip Flesh screamed like a mountain lion in pain and anger as he held his hand to his left ear- of which the eardrum had burst. Lashing out with his right hand, the size of a ham, he was caught off guard as Pretty Man seized the wrist and maneuvered it into an arm lock behind the older man's back. Heaving upward with all his might, he dislocated the extremity from its shoulder socket with a dull, sickening popping sound.

"Oh! Did you see that, Margaret? It appears that the young man has gained the advantage over the older man!" shouted Libbie.

Margaret moved in on Et-nah-wah-ruchta, her voice was thick and husky.

"What do you think about that?" asked Margaret.

"Touch me an' I kill you!" responded the startled Et-nah-wah-ruchta, as she spun around electrified, facing Margaret.

Poquerhienee had climbed twelve feet up the cottonwood tree and sat perched on a large branch, maintaining her balance by holding onto a smaller branch on either side of her. It seemed to her that the fight had swung decisively in Pretty Man's favor; she watched with hope and astonishment as he quickly wrenched the disjointed arm nearly full circle. No longer bound by the now useless arm, Teeth That Rip Flesh turned about face unexpectedly and lurched forward, grabbing the nose of Pretty Man with his pointed teeth and sheared it off.

"Threaten her again and I'll see to it that your husband is sent to Texas and that you move into my house!" hissed Elizabeth Custer in a sibilant warning to Et-nah-wah-ruchta.

Libbie advanced on Et-nah-wah-ruchta, massaging away the red welts that remained on her wrist. Leaning forward Elizabeth cautioned her maid servant with measured words, anger barely held in restraint.

"Now you listen to me Et-nah-wah-ruchta and you listen well. When those two rascals are finished killing each other in that creek, we will go back to the Custer House and you will help Margaret and myself prepare our meals and baths. I am utterly fatigued with this day's events, and poor Margaret is almost beside herself in wishing to egress from this abominable event. You are not to return home until you have ministered to the sufferings of Margaret and myself. Margaret will instruct you on the trivial details while I undress."

Distracted by the admonishment of Libbie, Et-nah-wah-ruchta turned her head quickly to the creek, the image of Teeth That Rip Flesh spitting an object from his mouth into the water reflected from the black pupil of her obsidian eyes.

Pretty Man thrust his hands to his face and stepped back, his left foot slipped on the surface of a smooth rock, causing him to go under the water unexpectedly. Teeth That Rip Flesh spat out the nose of Pretty Man into the water, where it was immediately seized by several small fish which fought over it before it disappeared. Teeth That Rip Flesh advanced uncertainly toward the point where Pretty Man had submerged. Poquerheinee swatted flies and gnats away from her sweaty face with one hand, as she held onto a tree branch with the other. Her small buttocks were seated firmly on a large branch as she watched the combat with mounting horror.

Teeth That Rip Flesh continued to scour the bed of the creek, feeling with his bare feet for Pretty Man, uncertain from which angle the next attack would ensue. A commotion from a short distance downstream prompted Teeth That Rip Flesh to look to his right. Poquerheinee could see from her eyrie that something had occurred downstream that was creating an uproar. Elizabeth Custer raised her opera glass to her eyes in order to see what was agitating the throng of Native Americans that were running toward the bend in the creek fifty yards downstream.

A village hetman, the same who had assumed command when the sachem fell to his death, approached the cottonwood tree where Poquerheinee sat perched. She watched as the villagers pulled the lifeless body of Pretty Man from the bend in the creek. She turned her head to where Teeth That Rip Flesh was wading ashore in knee deep water. His gait was unsteady and water dripped from his large, dangling penis as it swung from side to side. Without warning, Teeth That Rip Flesh collapsed into the water face down. No one rushed to help him as the spectators nearest heard the bubbles coughed from his lungs as he inhaled the water.

"This changes everything." Muttered Elizabeth to no one in particular.

"What has happened?" asked Margaret. "I want to know what is going on!"

Clearly Libbie was frustrated, and began gathering her things as she spoke sharply to Et-nah-wah-ruchta.

"What unseemly mirth is this?" asked Libbie of Et-nah-wah-ruchta, "To what end do you restrain the words from leaving your lips? Words which would beguile, and beggar us to stay at this wretched event, I'll wager!"

Et-nah-wah-ruchta responded to Libbie's statement by explaining to Margaret; "Both mens die. Arikawa from many days ride come from all aroun' to see creek fight, see Poquerheinee take buck. Now hetman tell Poquerheinee choose husband."

The three women watched as Poquerheinee descended from the tree and began arguing with the hetman. Both were gesticulating wildly, waving their arms and motioning with their hands.

"Go down there and discover what Poquerheinee decides, as Margaret and I prepare to depart." commanded Libbie.

"Oh Libbie! Do tell me we will not persist in our stay one moment more!" expostulated Margaret.

"We will leave with Et-nah-wah-ruchta in our company as soon as she returns. She approaches even now." placated Libbie.

The maid servant was excited and searched for the words to make the two white women understand what Poquerheinee demanded in this unusual situation.

"Poquerhienee say to hetman she take husband that win fightin' in creek. She say let all men fight in water, if they wanna plant face between thighs."

The trio of women looked to the creek banks and saw to their amazement several dozen young men stripping themselves of clothing, many of them were very drunk.

"Them men no have wives. All gonna fight in water for Poquerheinee."

Already there were several pairs of warriors engaged in combat, not waiting for the hetman to signal the go ahead. Others were entering the water.

One warrior, a big heavily tattooed brute, attacked another from behind in waist deep water, wrapping his arms around the victim's neck as he mounted him piggy back, scissoring his legs around the surprised man's waist. Dragging him under the water, he held him there. The muscles stood out in bold relief on either side of his neck as he strained to hold the man under.

"Well, all of that is fine and dandy, but we have to go now." retorted Libbie Custer.

The flank of the horse quivered and shook as a large, greenish horsefly bit deeply into its flesh. Et-nah-wah-ruchta watched the fighting with intensity as she untied the reins from the low hanging branch of the cottonwood tree.

"My goodness, Libbie! What if there are no men left among the village to provide the garrison with scouts and translators?" asked Margaret.

The feather weighted phaeton was a unique four wheeled English High Flyer which leaned slightly and righted itself as Libbie mounted the left side of the carriage.

"Good riddance." Libbie answered, "The preponderance is a menagerie of vagabonds and wastrels. Once the women have pulled the naked bodies of the men from the creek and dragged them to the garbage heap, those men will realize their life's fulfillment in the stomachs of their poor, starving dogs!"

Et-nah-wah-ruchta handed Libbie the reins as she climbed aboard the phaeton and positioned herself between the two ladies and resumed the reins. A skillful driver, she adroitly maneuvered the huge beast with a series of clicking sounds and set the beast bounding up the dirt road.

"Heeeyahhh!" Et-nah-wah-ruchta shouted as she plied the buggy whip.

The phaeton had four large spoked wheels; the rear wheels were substantially larger than those of the front. The springs were light and the body small. Everything that unnecessarily added weight had been intentionally omitted. The buggy was light, fast, and dangerous. It had no side panels but had a closed back with a calabash top that shielded the occupants from the sun. The firm yet comfortable leather seat was high backed and stuffed with horse hair. The back of Et-nah-wah-ruchta was outlined in sweat on the face of the tanned horsehide seat leather each time she leaned forward, yelling:

"Heeeyahhh!"

« Chapter Twenty One »

LIBBIE CUSTER SAT ON the leather club chair, her night gown buttoned up to her neck. She wore house shoes made of buffalo fur and her legs rested on a matching futon. Her hair was still wet from her bath and was brushed straight down. She sipped strong black coffee from an ornate china coffee cup. Elizabeth would have been in bed, deep in exhausted slumber, were it not for the sight unfolding before her eyes. Et-nah-wah-ruchta brushed the tangles from the mane of auburn hair that cascaded over the well-formed shoulders of Margaret, who was clothed only in a towel and shivered both from being freshly bathed and from unimaginable excitement. Et-nah-wah-ruchta was fully dressed. The play of muscles on her back and shoulder blades with each stroke of the hairbrush were hidden by the doe skin pull over dress, which was adorned with beads sewn into the leather garment in intricate designs.

"Ouch, you sadistic beast!" Margaret shouted, exaggerating her expostulation to frighten and intimidate Et-nah-wah-ruchta.

Margaret stood up, turning about and facing Et-nah-wah-ruchta. She allowed the towel to fall from her shoulders. The contrast between the physiques of the two women were profound; the tan, athletic figure of the Native American woman bore little similarity to the full bosomed European American woman that faced her.

"I have never beheld such fierce beauty" murmured Margaret, as she placed her hands on either side of the Cree's head, twisting her fingers in the wet, black hair.

"Dog!" shouted Et-nah-wah-ruchta. "I told you once, sister of Elizabeth Custer, if you touch me I kill you!"

Margaret stepped back with an "Unghh!" The Cree had slapped the large, pendulous breasts of the white woman with a clenched fist, and it had knocked the breath from her.

Et-nah-wah-ruchta lunged into the surprised Margaret, who crossed her arms over her breasts which were engorged from the vicious blow of the Indian woman. The Cree (Arikawa) wielded her hands like claws, her right arm describing an arc as she sought to rake Margaret's face with her taloned fingernails.

"Bitch!" hissed Libbie as she grabbed the younger woman's hair from behind and jerked her head back. Margaret lost no time regaining her composure and seized the advantage offered by the intrusion of her sister in law.

The moment was interrupted by furious knocking at one of the front doors.

"Mrs. Custer! Mrs. Custer!" a voice shouted from the veranda of the home.

"Now don't you two do another thing until my return!" expostulated the exasperated general's wife.

"What is it you want?!" demanded the annoyed Elizabeth Custer as she flung open the door.

Dressed in her full length robe, buttoned up to the neck, she betrayed severe annoyance to the foul smelling, old soldier-a habitual ne'er do well and alcoholic who did chores for the Custers.

"I'm sorry Ma'am, but the Far West steamboat is coming down the creek and is within eyesight of the fort. There are many wounded from the 7th on board and mention of a disaster was sent by runner. You said you wanted to be told."

"What are you saying?" responded Libbie.

"Some kinda disaster, ma'am. Really ain't heard too much more'n that, ma'am!"

Libbie saw the drunkard's eyes looking beyond her, and into the bedroom where the sounds of glass breaking and of women cursing could be heard.

"Is there somethin' goin' on? Ma'am? I hear somethin' back there in that yonder room. Maybe I oughta go have a look-see…"

"If you step one foot in my house, my husband will have you tied to the wheel of the wagon and bull whipped!" threatened Libbie Custer, there was venom in her voice, and hatred. Hatred of the foul smelling miscreant that stood before her, his uniform filthy, hair unwashed and beard unshaven. She involuntarily gave a start and stepped back when she saw several large fleas emerge and disappear into the scroungy, graying beard.

"Well, there was another somethin' that ah forgot to relate to you, Mrs. Custer!" the washed out, poor excuse for a soldier managed to divulge. He smiled, releasing the fetid breath from rotted, decaying teeth.

"You get out! Go on! I don't want to hear anymore!" responded Libbie, her voice was shrill, and carried with it the tone of worry. She had looked into the blurred, cataractic eyes of the wastrel and had seen a premonition of her most horrifying fear.

"Why, it's about yore husban' ma'am - General Custer!"

"Go on! Get out, I said! Get!" Libbie's voice was frantic, the noises emanating from the bed room ceased.

"They sayin' he done gone an' gotten his self killed! That's what they sayin' ma'am! It's just somethin' awful! An' I mean to offer my sincere condolences."

The eyes of the stuffed animals that adorned the walls seemed to be alive with a horrible understanding...

About the Author

William Sumrall has lived in an interesting array of places. Although his pedigree hails from Mississippi for many generations, he was the first to break that trend when he was born in Florida. From Rhode Island to Alaska, William (he likes to be called Bill) has met an interesting mix of people and seen many fascinating places.

After finishing high school in Texas, he served three years in Germany, having gotten to know friends and seen places that add to his experiences in life. Upon completion of his enlistment, he attended a junior college in North Texas where he graduated with an AA degree. He went on to take a BA with a major in Spanish at a university in Southeastern Oklahoma.

Not content to settle down, the yearning for adventure could not be resisted, and he re-enlisted as a rifleman in the Marine Corps. When he was 30 years old he married his wife, Maria. By then he was a sergeant in a rifle company. With his re-enlistment completed, he moved with his wife to rural Southeastern Oklahoma, where he works as a nurse at a rural hospital.

A few of his many hobbies include fishing for catfish, although these days he always releases the fish; he has it not in his heart to hurt them. An avid amateur herpetologist, he has kept many snakes and lizards as pets, and maintains an interesting array of aquatic life in his aquariums as well. Not limiting his peculiar interests in the Natural Sciences to the worldly, he also has a ten inch Newtonian reflecting telescope, which he has trained to the heavens on numerous occasions. As a matter of fact, he has located and identified every Messier Object in the night sky using antiquated star charts.

Bill has a proclivity toward the shooting sports, as well; he has a fine assortment of handguns with which he likes to practice on his pistol range.

Always having been a voracious reader, his delvings have spanned the gamut of adventure, including mountain climbing, polar exploration, SCUBA diving, Amazon exploration and closest to his heart - Military History.

While certainly not a Renaissance man, he certainly is widely read and speculative.